I0788776

MARRIED BY STARFALL

ARRANGED MARRIAGES OF THE FAE

MEG COWLEY

Eldarkin Publishing Limited
United Kingdom
© 2022 Meg Cowley
www.megcowley.com

ISBN 9781915731012

Dust jacket cover design © Franziska Stern 2022
Under jacket cover design © Amira Naval 2022

❀ Created with Vellum

to Pelenor
N
W
E
S
cabin
stone circle
kassimir's keep
barrows
THE WILDEWOOD

A TALE OF STARFALL—EXCERPT

When night's zenith stills, all delight
that fated twain shall join on Starfall night.
With the passing of gods high 'bove,
that fair celestial's true mortal love
shall return to heaven and star.
In her arms he shall rest e'ermore, afar
from the cares of the fading lands
blessed with grace by her fair, undying hands.

CHAPTER ONE

To enter the Wildewood was beyond foolish. To seek the continent's most feared fae sorcerer within its borders? Certain death. Venya stared up at the tangle of trees before her—unnaturally thick after the bare winter woods on the other side of the river. Her sweaty palms slid inside her leather gloves, but her mouth felt so dry her tongue clove to its roof, thick and clumsy.

The evergreen Wildewood swallowed the road in darkness. She could hardly see a hundred yards ahead. Foreboding prickled on the back of Venya's neck and a stray breeze brushed her face, pushing her back as though nature itself warned her against this forsaken place.

She had not come so far, only to turn tail at the sight of her destination, all for fear of the spectres haunting her mind. Her mother's life hung in the balance—she could not fail again. Familiar guilt overpowered her apprehension. Venya plunged her horse into the dark forest before she could dwell upon it any longer.

Her breath frosted before her, a visible reminder of the turn of the season. She breathed what little magic she could spare into heating her hands—they were stiff upon the reins after so many hours of riding. Her jaw clenched to stop it chattering—it felt too loud an interruption to the blanket silence of the place. She did not want to shatter that quiet. Strange howls laced the distant air and things rustled through the surrounding forest, unseen. This was not the place to attract attention.

She was far from her homeland of Pelenor now, treading territories she had only seen before on maps. The Wilde-wood was aptly named. The road south had become little more than a winding, rutted track, and even that was a generous stretch to describe it as the forest encroached upon it, trying to reclaim it. Gnarled roots tangled through the mud, threatening to trip her steed.

The excruciating delay of their slow pace grated upon her already wrought nerves. Every crashing hoofbeat was a hammer strike upon her heart.

Too slow.

You'll be too late.

She's going to die.

It's all your fault.

The punishing inner monologue plagued every waking moment, draining her focus, but Venya could not outrun it. She glanced up. The canopy was too thick to see the sky—no chance of guiding them by the stars or the sun. It was perpetual gloaming and her eyes stung from the dingy murk of it. The miserable nature of the place kept the sun out, as though those boughs spread high above her were determined no light should grace the forest floor.

All around, the forest grew thick. The petrichor scent of that perpetually damp place was rich in her nose and so thick she could almost taste it. It was still so emerald, the predomi-nantly evergreen forest punctuated by violent shades of fire and blood as the rare deciduous trees ceded to the turn of the year and clung to the last of their leaves.

She would have to find a safe place to make camp soon. Venya gritted her teeth. She had left the nearest inn behind three days ago at the borders of Valtivar, the last civilised land before her destination. Tonight, the terrain looked so deeply unfriendly—uneven, rocky, root-covered ground, and no proper shelter—that stopping on the road might be her only choice, for she had seen nowhere that could otherwise be suitable.

Venya did not relish it. The journey sapped her and her very bones ached. It had been two weeks now, and the urgency that had first driven her had faded, tempered by irritable tiredness and a healthy respect for the gigantic predatory tracks they had encountered crisscrossing the road.

That road felt entirely too vulnerable and open to rest upon. They had encountered no fell beasts, and Venya intended to keep it that way. She had shrouded their scents with magic and done what she could to dampen the sound of their passage, but even so, an uneasy itch niggled at the back of her neck. Were they being watched, hunted, even now? It set her on edge. She had not managed to sleep more than a few minutes here and there since leaving the comfort of the inn.

Crack.

The horse's hoof struck hard road.

Venya glanced down and frowned. A stone road. Ahead, it bent, and when she turned the corner, it widened into a discernible road once more. *Are we through the other side?* It couldn't be. She thought there was at least another day of travel. Mind, the maps of this area were few, and she was not convinced of their accuracy. Perhaps she was mistaken.

She glanced behind her. The thickness of the trees seemed to retreat a little, that choke hold on all light diminishing ever so slightly as the horse plodded downhill, each step painfully loud to her ears. Here, the trees were not so thick, and ahead, they retreated entirely from the roadside.

So distracted from her surroundings by her own internal flagellation… she had stumbled upon something malign that she had not anticipated.

Barrows lined the way.

A dozen mounds stretched into a rising mist. An *unnaturally* rising mist, one that materialised as they approached.

A chill wormed its way down Venya's back at the same moment that the horse stopped of its own will, almost between the first two barrows. They towered—half as high again as Venya seated on the horse's back.

"Come on, Boy," Venya whispered. The horse did not budge. She slipped her gloves off and tucked them into her belt.

It was deadly silent. The quiet that warned of danger, for all beasts had fled. She sent her senses far beyond herself —nothing.

Around them, that mist rose between the cobbles. Boy pranced on the spot and tossed his head, the whites of his eyes visible as it twisted around his hooves.

She felt that unnatural sensation, too. Something cold slithering over her senses. An instinctual fear telling her *bad, run, go*. Her hands clenched so tightly around Boy's reins that they were numb—frozen like the rest of her body in a moment of fear—before she forced herself to unlock.

Fear would get her nowhere. She had faced enough beasts and grimoires to know she could do it. She had to. Her mother counted on her. If Venya did not succeed—or worse still, died upon the road—her mother was doomed.

That spurred her into action, more so than worry for her own safety. Venya dug her heels into Boy once—and then harder still, harder than she would otherwise have done when he refused. That jab had him skittering forward, though he sidestepped too, showing his displeasure at his mistress for forcing him to move. Venya fought the reins with him, urging him forward.

"Come on, Boy," she urged him softly. They had to get out of this place. It was a place of death and fell magic and she had no desire to linger past nightfall where who knew what fell creatures would emerge from the forest. *Or those barrows,* her mind suggested unhelpfully.

A shudder ran through her. Her breath caught in her chest, the instinctive fear rising internally seizing her lungs, and she forced herself to breathe, scanning her surroundings.

Deadly silent. Not a beast stirred, not a creature broke for cover, not a bird dared to sing. Even the wind had dropped.

What is this place?

She had read of places like this, though seen few. An old burial site perhaps, long forgotten and longer still abandoned. Not to be disturbed, in any case. Not all graves were mortal. Not all graves were empty, either.

She saw no entry into the barrows, but that did not mean that there were none. Beasts often lurked within such places, ready to catch stray travellers unaware on the road. Venya gritted her teeth against the intrusion of her imagination. How unhelpfully vivid it was, serving her such distasteful morsels when she least needed them.

Now the fog had reached Boy's ankles, so unnaturally thick Venya could barely see the cobbles beneath his hooves. Cold air wound down the nape of her neck. Her breath caught at the unpleasant, frigid moistness there, and the other scent that laced the air, of something long dead.

The barrows ahead, nearing on either side, appeared to float amongst that sea of swirling white. Old stones littered them, moss-covered, weather-stained, and with swirling lichens adorning them. Ferns burst in messy clusters atop the ones nearest. Upon the next, a gnarled and stunted tree grew, its bloodred leaves scarce with dark arms stabbing into the sky, many fingered and threatening.

Thud. Thud. Thud. The pounding of her heart elevated again as Boy's steel shoes rang upon the now invisible cobbles.

They passed the first barrows. Overgrown and small, these looked ancient, undisturbed. The next were slightly bigger. Ahead, amongst that ever-rising mist, were at least half a dozen more on either side.

She wondered how long they had been there, but she had no inclination to linger for an answer. Not with the prickling taste of sorcery bitter upon her tongue. It laced the very air around her.

Has some fell creature made this place its home? Have I unwittingly stumbled into its den? She sent her senses far out around her, reaching for life, for magic, for any sign of impending danger.

The closest creature she sensed was at the very edge of her consciousness—something small and weak. No threat. It truly seemed all life had fled this forsaken place—or avoided it entirely, perhaps. But nothing of sorcery.

Then it flared, blooming behind her. It was no brightness, no light of life, no pull from the energy stream of magic running through the world around her. This was no source. It was a drain. Dark and vicious.

The hiss of metal drawing was the only warning her earthly body received. Venya turned instinctively, twisting in Boy's saddle, and gasped a sharp intake of breath. A dark figure loomed behind her. Even high on Boy's back, it almost came to the same height as her.

Half ethereal, half corporeal, she could not tell whether it was formed or spectre in the hazing air. Black and amorphous, its cloak seemed wreathed of shadow itself, draping over a tall, thin form, and no face amidst the cowl could she discern—save for two glowing, red shards where eyes ought to have been.

A barrow wight.

CHAPTER TWO

Kassimir stalked through the trees, every step in silence and shadow, following the scent of magic. It was not his. His own curdled through him, angry and raw. At least he would have something to take his fury out on that day, even though it would not distract from the primal fear he did not want to admit to.

The wards were breaking. He knew what that meant. When they ended, so too would he.

That dark thing inside him writhed with glee at the prospect of freedom once more.

Kass shoved it deeper. It did not subside willingly, fingers of darkness slipping through the cracks, resisting him until at last he had it contained, seams pressed together and cracks papered over somewhere deep inside him. Even the exertion of that once simple act had him stopping to brace against a tree.

The tree shuddered at his touch. It felt what lurked inside him. An antithesis to life.

He prowled on when the nausea and dizziness subsided, his teeth gritted. Ahead lay the breach. Today, it was visible.

It was not only the unseen magic rippling through the air which had been sundered, but the physical plane too.

The very earth had been ripped apart, stones the size of bears cast wide, and trees torn from their roots, their mangled carcasses twisting upon the ground. In the very centre of the maelstrom, a pit. He did not look into its depths —he knew he would not see their extent. This would tunnel into the bowels of the stone and earth foothills.

An acidic, sulphurous aroma hung over the place, bitter and choking as ash. Kass paused, as utterly still as any predator, and sent his senses out into the gloaming. Darkness fell and the forest ought to have been full of life, but there was only silence and the threat of what lurked unseen. Had they retreated into the dark bowels of the tunnel with daylight? Would they come with the turning of day to night? Or had they already roamed free and far, devastating his lands and the surrounding Wildewood?

A whisper.

So quiet he would not have heard it, but for his preternatural fae ears picking up that tiny ripple through the air.

Kass gritted his teeth and grinned wildly. *In the hole, then.*

They whispered promises of destruction come the darkness, and that was moments away. Soon, the last of the sun's light would dip over the horizon, and then these denizens would be free to wreak destruction until morning. Not on his watch. Not whilst he still drew breath, doomed though he was.

With fluid grace, his hands rising and fingertips splaying, he turned upon that yawning maw, building a wall of magic. And, as they slithered forth, indistinct dark shapes, voids of light against the dark lands, he unleashed the tide.

At once, night turned to day. Blinding light emanated from him, illuminating the clearing and exposing the pit of

Darkyn demons writhing in the bottom. Their painful shrieks cut through him to the core, slicing through his hearing with savage pain, but Kass only threw back his head and laughed, a roar of defiance, taking out his fury on the dark scum before him. They could not stand in his way.

Fire blasted from his outstretched palms, ripping them to shreds until all that remained in that clearing was the tatters of their beings, floating on the breeze. They faded into shadow and silence. And then, there was nothing.

He held that threat of power a moment longer than necessary, just to make sure. His sorcery found no further targets. Kass let it slip away, and the clearing faded to darkness. It took a moment for his eyes to adjust to the night again. He breathed heavily, though not with exertion, more the rush of it, and his brow wrinkled. That had not satisfied him. Why had it not satisfied him? He still felt the niggle of displeasure and discomfort. This had been no distraction from his true problem.

That darkness slithered inside him once more. He slammed a wall against it and, reluctantly, it ceased. He sighed, but it was more a growl that emerged.

With the hole now cleansed of the demon filth that had tunnelled up from the bowels of the mountains, he backfilled it, fuelled by unnatural strength, magic, and ire. He dragged trees thrice his size, rocks as big as he, and moved mounds of earth using a shattered branch as a shovel into that hole until what had been a dark slash in the earth was now a mound of chaos. It was a mess, but it was blocked, at least.

Kass looked skyward. The moon shimmered between banked clouds. From the change in the air, snow would come soon. It was a later hour than he had anticipated, and he still had the wards to reset.

Sinking deep into that part of himself that thrummed

with the vibrant energy of a wellspring, he plucked at the magic, forming it viscerally into the net that encompassed his lands in a giant arc. They kept out the worst beasts from the Wildewood—and the Darkyn, most of the time. The repairs were becoming more frequent. He cracked his neck and shoved that thought aside as he wove the delicate net, golden threads of light warming the cold, dark forest. He found the sundering and melded it together, making it whole until the breach, ten times his width and thrice his height, was repaired.

Slowly, that golden net faded from the visible plane, but he felt it there, unseen. Protecting him again. A shame it could not protect him from himself—and the Darkyn demon slowly devouring him from within.

Frustration jabbed at him once more, born of desperation. He would not go meekly or willingly to his death. There had to be a way.

"There isn't," came the insidious crooning reply from that demon inside him.

He jabbed mental daggers into it, and screeching with discomfort, it retreated into that internal vault.

Kass scanned the forest around him. Sound already filtered closer. The creatures of the forest instinctively avoided creatures such as the Darkyn, and they knew when such darkness had gone, and it was safe to return. That was as good a sign as any that his work there was done.

A breeze picked up, and Kass wrinkled his nose. On the wind, something fetid drifted… something like death.

And then a scream shattered the night.

CHAPTER THREE

*V*enya's stomach flipped and her heart stuttered. Paralysed with fear, that instant felt as though it lasted a lifetime as she took in the full horror of the wight.

It raised one of those spindle arms, revealing hands of mottled, withered, grey skin, so old and dead they were hardly more than bone. It gripped a sword of cold, blue-grey metal, the long blade of which was sharp, jagged, and cruel. That earthy wet scent shifted, and with it now came the old, cold, smell of decay and things long dead.

A screech rang forth from the wight. It was the grate of metal, the bray of a donkey, and the thousand anguished cries of the dead—so heinous that Venya screamed. Boy surged into motion, pulling Venya away just as that fell blade sliced down. It caught nothing but air, carving through the fog.

Venya twisted in her saddle, drawing her dagger. The blade felt utterly insubstantial against the long sword of the wight, but Venya had nothing else but her elven magic with which to face it.

Fight or run?

She had moments to make the choice. She turned back, seeing that the wight gained upon her. Never mind that Boy was at full canter. It *flew* through the fog behind her, sword outstretched. They would not be able to outrun this. She had no option but to fight for both of their lives.

Seconds stretched and raced. What did she know of wights? All those years and all those books, they must have taught her *something*! The thought was desperate as she scrabbled at the closing walls of her own panicking mind to find something.

Light!

"Wights feed upon life and hate the light, fear these creatures 'midst the night."

The fragment of an old rhyme, read long ago, drifted through her mind. She snatched at it, but it was gone—leaving behind an answer she had no choice but to cling to.

Venya held her dagger in one hand and dropped the reins, raising her clawed hand and drawing on that well of power inside her. Focusing the power through her palm, she sent a thundering bolt of light at the wight. It struck home, and the wight screeched anew, the sound so grating that Boy staggered under her and Venya screamed, her ears lancing with pain at the cacophony.

The wight fell back and Venya wrenched at Boy's reins, forcing him to stop and turn. It would do them no good to try to flee.

Her mouth was dry, her clammy palms sliding over the smooth leather as she dropped the reins once more, steering Boy with her legs, and urged him back towards that crumpled mess sinking through the fog.

The wight rose anew, surging to full height before her. Her heart stopped. Its arms stretched wider than she was tall. She rode straight for its clutching embrace.

It raised that dark blade anew. Boy darted to one side. Venya met the skittering steel with a blow that felt as though it had shattered her arm in its socket, the power of the beast and the weight of the blade so much more than she had expected. More than she could fight. It knocked the very breath from her.

They charged past, back the way they had come. Boy's hooves thundered on those cobbles, each hoofbeat jarring through her. Venya wheeled him around again, tossing her long plait out of the way and hating the way her cloak tangled her limbs, dragging her down.

Light crackled in her palm, laced with fire. She sucked all the energy she could afford to give it and sent it into the back of the wight as it turned. That light-fire caught, setting the ethereal cloak alight and skittering across its umbral surface.

The wight's shriek cut to her core. Nausea overwhelmed her, and Venya fought the urge to vomit. Boy pranced backwards, nostrils flaring, mouth foaming, eyes rolling—the beast was half wild, and she was no master horsewoman. She could not hope to control him for much longer.

Light illuminated the barrows surrounding them, her magic fire blazing brightly amongst the looming dark. And then it vanished. Snuffed out with the scent of burning fabric, something deeper and more unpleasant.

The stench of sulphur rolled across her. Venya gagged. In the sudden absence of light, her eyes struggled, picking out only the starkest contrast of shadow against fog. She blazed light down the length of her dagger, using it almost as a torch as she raised it anew and Boy reared—just as the wight's sword came down upon Boy's neck. Venya wrenched Boy's reins to the side but could not avoid it.

"No!" she screamed as that blade struck and bit deep into his thick neck. Boy let out a screech, pain lacing the poor beast's voice, but there was no time to lament. Boy's movement gave out and then she was falling. In a moment, she would be crushed beneath his bulk and at the wight's mercy.

Venya slipped her feet free from the stirrups, and, thanking her elven grace, vaulted away. Her cloak caught the air, rippling and folding around her. The fall was awkward as she sought to avoid Boy's thrashing movements, being impaled upon her own dagger, the roughest of landings on the cobbles below, and the encroaching wight.

She slammed into the cobbles. Winded, she could do nothing but lie there, dazed for a moment and blanketed in that fog. The ground shuddered next to her as Boy fell, still screaming, and his hot blood spattered her exposed hands and cheeks.

"*No!*" she sobbed, but winded, it came out as a half croak. She forced herself to move, lungs burning. Venya rolled onto her side. Then over onto all fours. Her nails tore on those cobbles and cold bled through her palms as she scrabbled. Up onto her knees, she pushed. The wight loomed before her, crouching over Boy's form. The horse lashed out—by luck his hoof just missed shattering her thigh—but his movements grew weaker.

The wight *fed* on Boy, draining his fading life.

Nausea roiled inside Venya. She staggered to her feet. "You cannot have him!" she cried, desperate to believe he was not yet lost. She could not be responsible for another death. She launched forward, blazing dagger outstretched and light-fire burning in her palm once more.

It blazed brighter than before, fed by desperation, ragged hope, and fear. She thrust it forward with a roar that would befit a beast more than an elven maiden and launched herself upon the creature with all thoughts of safety gone—only survival. If she did not give her all, they would both die—and her mother too.

The wight turned to meet her. Its blade lay embedded in Boy's neck. Boy lay too still. Despair rose with an angry sob in Venya as her light snuffed out again, her blazing dagger the only insulation against the dark. A wave of sulphur and smoke washed over her again. She coughed and fell back, circling the wight warily. Her heart hammered. Her mind raced.

Venya swung the dagger at the wight, but he knocked her grasp aside with a bony fist that jarred her wrist. A cry of alarm burst from her chest.

The light on her dagger sputtered.

Cast in the flickers, a deeper shadow rose behind the wight. Her heart stopped. *Another wight?* She was done for. Utterly doomed. With the quenching of her hope, so too the light upon Venya's dagger faltered, plunging her into twilight lit only by the inadequate glow of the baleful moon far above.

Her foot slipped upon a loose cobble. She looked down instinctively and fought to catch her balance, her concentration dropping from the wight. She staggered up once more, and her heart stopped. The wight's cowl was as close to her face as a lover ready to press a kiss upon her lips.

A cold hand closed under her neck and cut the breath from her.

The freeze of death seeped from that point of contact as she looked into the dark hood of the wight and saw only her end there upon the smiling skull within.

CHAPTER FOUR

No one should have been in the Wildewood—no one in their right mind, in any case—and yet that female scream had been very real. Kass moved upon instinct, disintegrating into shadow and wind as he slipped through the fabric of the world much faster than even his fae feet could carry him, to the source of that sound.

He realised where it drew him. To the wight road. A forsaken place as any in the Wildewood. What foolish dolt had come this way? He would have left them to their well-deserved fate had it not been for the threat that the wights presented. If they walked the world once more, it meant the darkness the Darkyn had brought seeped out further than their little tunnel. Perhaps there were more. Whatever the cause, things awoke in the forest that ought to have been long dead.

Near the road Kass slowed, stepping from ether and shadows onto fog-wreathed cobbles. They were jagged under his feet, an invisible hazard waiting to trip him, for that fog was so thick it was impenetrable, and it wound around his shins as though trying to claim him too. Several dark bulks loomed ahead on the road between the barrows.

Death called him towards it. A wight lurked there, life bleeding from its first victim, a horse upon the road. The beast was doomed. Kass barely felt any life left in it, just a weak, erratic, and fading flutter. Life bloomed ahead, though. Death too. A contradiction of bright light and yawning void locked together.

Kass raced forward, ravenous fire molten in his blood as he shot towards the wight, drawing a dark blade of the only material capable of slaying what was already dead. Into the barrow wight's back he slammed that blade, wreathing the dark shadow-metal in fire. It penetrated to the core of the wight, which let out such an unearthly shriek, it felt as though Kass's bones would shatter from the strain of bearing it. Kass wrenched the blade free and retreated.

He saw a flash of terrified eyes from the wight's victim—a female elf—before the wight threw her to the floor and rose. She landed with a crunch and did not move. She would have to wait.

The wight rose and turned on him. Inside the depths of its cowl, he saw only single-minded destruction. Its sword skittered across the cobbles, its tip dragging on the stone. The wight raised the weapon, turning on him—and Kass sensed other blots around him. Dearths of life that signalled more wights attracted by the promise of such bright and blazing life for prey. Two. Three. A fourth distant but closing in.

"Go back to your rest," he snarled at it, and dived forward. The wight was insubstantial as he slammed into it, half ethereal and half corporeal. His blade pinned it as they tumbled together back onto a mound. He drove the full force of his weight into that dark dagger, until it was hilt-deep in the wight's chest, drowned from sight by its shadowy rags. His other hand clasped onto a bony wrist, and the cold of death seared into his palm, bringing with it a throb of pain to his forehead.

The wight writhed under him, that scream coming from no mouth, but shattering through him, the sound of dozens of mortals and fae, elves and beasts meeting their end. Kass held firm, gritting his teeth and roaring against that pain. The wight crumpled under him, around that savage cut, disintegrating into nothing until all that remained were shadows that sank into the barrow beneath him.

Kass sprang to his feet, muscles screaming, his hand throbbing savagely from where it had gripped the wight. Three more approached. Kass took quick stock. The horse was lost. The female, whoever she was, would be too if Kass did not intervene—and if he did not, the wights would take her life force and grow all the stronger for it.

He roared his defiance and skidded down the barrow, launching at her still form. She was barely visible, a small lump of an island drowning in the depths of that malevolent mist.

Passing the horse, Kass took what little life remained from it as gently as he could. Its end at the wights' hands would be worse, a slow and unimaginable pain as it hovered on the border between life and death for as long as they wished to feed on it. A merciful and clean end he could give it—and did. It shuddered and was still. What little remained of that horse's life would aid the saviour of its mistress.

Kass crouched over her still form. He could still feel life inside her—and magic too—weak and sluggish. *An elf.* He had more questions, but no time to ask them.

The wights drew closer, blots of darkness against the night sky. Kass had that kernel of life from the horse and the seething mess of his own magic, already depleted by the Darkyn. He sucked it all up, building that crescendo, higher than he had for the demons in the tunnel, and when the wights drew close enough, let it out in a giant blast. A wall of light incinerated them, rippling outwards, lighting the forest around them with such shocking brilliance that even the trees bent away from the light. And then it faded.

Gone were the wights and any trace of their imprint. Silent were the barrows. The fog sank into the cobbles as he watched, like a tide retreating, lapping around the cracks and then sinking beyond sight.

What remained was peace, darkness, and her.

Kass scooped her into his arms, wrapped in the tangle of her cloak. She was feather light, so fragile he feared he might break her—and yet, she had survived, somehow, where her horse had fallen, until his arrival.

His magic was depleted, but the trickle remaining hummed as it sensed the answering resonance inside her. He should have left her there. What business was it of his if she chose to foolishly endanger herself by traversing the Wilde-wood? He did not tolerate such idiocy, and besides which, he did not entertain visitors. A silly notion if ever there was one. And yet, he was not so lost to cowardice that he would knowingly turn his back upon her. She was clearly in no state to fend for herself. To do so would be to have her death on his hands. He could not bear another.

It meant nothing. Less than nothing. He could not absolve himself with some small kindness to her. It would not even wipe clean the edges of the stain upon his soul. He would heal her and turn her away. It was better that way.

And so, Kassimir took her into shadow and wind, back to his home in the heart of the Wildewood.

CHAPTER FIVE

The tower seemed a fitting place for her. Far from his quarters and safely out of his business. Kass laid her gently on the double bed there, resting her head softly on the plump pillow. He illuminated the lamps with a swirl of magic.

"Kass?" Pata had found him already. Typical. Pata somehow always knew what happened in Kass's domain.

Kass turned to the black panther, a construct of his own making. "We have a guest. Find her clothes and ensure she has what she needs, please."

Pata, one of few words, merely inclined his head and slipped away.

In the soft, warm light, the elf maiden looked pale and vulnerable. It tugged something internally. Kass tucked a stray lock of raven hair away from her face behind her pointed ear, feeling on edge about the intimacy of such a gesture with a complete stranger. He made no move to undress her, save to unclasp her cloak, so it did not strangle her as she rested.

Bared before him, he saw the wightmark upon her neck, a

patch of silver skin in the shape of the wight's bony hand where it had gripped her. He shuddered. Had it not been for the good fortune of him hearing her scream and finding her, she would already be lost to them.

As it was, the wightmark had leached some of the life from her. It would take a little while for the mark to fade, even for a magic-touched body like hers that was quicker to heal than most. Death was reluctant to be cheated.

He was utterly spent. What he had, he ought to have saved for himself, but he found himself holding his palm over her neck. He pushed healing magic into her, bending close to watch glittering sparks catch on her skin and sink into her throat. This close, he scented the salty sweat of the road on her—and the tang of fear too—plus that lingering undertone of death.

He passed his hands over her, finding an injury in her wrist, a fracture that he healed with some effort given his bone-deep exhaustion, but nothing else physical. A sigh of relief escaped him. She would survive—she needed rest, yes, but she would suffer no lasting effects. He cleared his throat and straightened. *Gather yourself, you fool.* It was not like him to care, after all. Why was he troubled?

The demon stirred deep down. His own strength depleted, he did not have the will or might to stay it. Drawn to her life like a moth to a flame, it circled and rose.

"Oh yes. She will be delicious."

"You can't have her, Ozul," he snarled to it. He felt it savouring her essence, and it made him nauseous. "She's..." he was about to say *mine*, even though he could not say why. She was a stranger. Nothing more.

The demon laughed softly. It had seen the slip. It perceived every deep and jagged part of his soul, fused with him as it was. *"Can't I?"*

"No." Kass bared his teeth. He clenched his fists, but what could he do? *I can hardly pummel that which is already inside me, entwined inextricably with my own soul.*

"Not for much longer."

Kass closed his eyes against that, but he could not deny it. The demon would not be contained much longer. Not as the bonds fusing them crumbled. He had bound the thing once. He could not do so again. Not with the cost of it. He clamped down on the memory of fire and death.

"Yes, you can." Again, the demon laughed softly. *"Only, you are too much of a coward to do it, Kassimir, and I am glad of that, for I yearn to roam free once more."*

Heat prickled at Kass's eyes, and his voice was raw when he answered. "You already had your fill of death and devastation. Was that not enough for you?"

"It will never be enough. Come Starfall, I will be free. I will devour you."

Slowly and painfully. Kass already had the promise of it. He had kept Ozul bound for centuries now. He had already seen its fantasies played out in his worst nightmares, of how it would repay him for that long captivity and starvation.

"I will devour everything you hold dear." All of his creatures, all of his constructs, it would take their magic to bolster its own power.

"I will devour everything in my path until I am unstoppable, just like before. This time, you shall not stop me."

Kass's head bowed with the weight of those promises. With the weight of the burden burying him. It grew so large now, he could hardly breathe. Starfall. He had less than three weeks left—and still, no answer.

The female on the bed stirred and mumbled an indecipherable syllable before she trailed into silence again. So fragile, she had hovered close to that border between life and death at first. He had drawn her back towards life, without even thinking. It had been the right thing to do. He had acted on instinct. Perhaps he was a better male than he gave himself credit for.

He huffed a mirthless laugh. *No, you're not, Kassimir.*

She had been doomed to die. Without his intervention, she would already be gone. *Could I...?*

The thought curdled, so heinous it sank into his subconscious, so cowardly he could not give words to it. If she had been doomed to die anyway, could she still serve that purpose and save him from a fate worse than his own death at the hands of the demon Darkyn that resided within him?

Ozul cackled with glee inside him. If he did that, it would mean he could bind the demon again. The demon had no mirth for that—only the painful moral dilemma he now found himself in.

Ozul crooned, *"You'll never do it. You're a coward."*

Yet, if Kass did not sacrifice the female who had dropped from the heavens like a gift upon his doorstep, he would doom himself, not to mention countless others.

CHAPTER SIX

*V*enya drifted through the dark. The deathly cold of that freezing hand burned like ice-fire upon her neck. Yet, in the haze of nothingness, she could have sworn big, warm hands grasped her, tucked her into a warm, safe, firm hold, smoothing away the visceral terror and despair she had felt mere moments ago, and lifted her away.

That touch welcomed her so deeply she felt something instinctively ease. Death's embrace was more comfortable than she imagined, homely and warm. It swept away her guilt at failing, numbing all her feelings and the pain with a balm so deep it sunk into her very bones.

THIS WAS NOT DEATH. She *hurt*. Some part of her realised that life still awaited outside the diminished sphere of her existence. More hurt, too. This did not pain her as much as it ought to. The mark of death upon her neck was nothing more than an irritating tingle now. The jar her wrist had taken was now just a small ache. But she felt the shadow of pain from the fight in every muscle of her body, as though it were there but beyond what she could perceive.

Had she imagined the warm, safe presence taking her away? Was it simply relief at not dying? Perhaps she had passed quickly. Was *this* death? That was too much to contemplate.

The memories surfaced alongside physical sensations. The horror of it. Again and again. The wight. The attack. Her desperate defence. Boy. Boy falling. Boy… *no*. She could not go that far. Could not think it. Too painful. She retreated again into the safe cocoon of nothing, soothed by the hand upon hers and the warm, damp cloth upon her brow.

VENYA ROSE CLOSER to the surface this time. That pain was not so far away. It was intense enough to anchor her to what felt like a physical world. One in which she had survived. Every muscle, every bone groaned. Her wrist throbbed with a beat of its own, and her neck burned. Even breathing hurt, the rise and fall of her chest too painful to take anything more than a shallow breath.

She let out a soft moan and cracked her gritty, swollen eyes open.

A male stared down at her, so broad of shoulder he took up almost her entire field of vision.

She shrank back into a soft bed instinctively, before she saw the cloth in his raised hand and made the connection. *Is this who has been tending me?*

She thought it had been her imagination. Perhaps a figment of death itself. But this very much felt real—the warm coverlet beneath her hands, soft pillow beneath her head, fire crackling in a hearth somewhere to her right.

His brows furrowed at the movement. He splayed both hands, palms facing her. A gesture of peace. "I mean you no harm, lady," he said in a low, deep voice that stirred something inside her.

Venya's eyes slipped shut and tears of relief pricked. *I'm alive,* she thought with wonder. And then, *how?* That wight had had her by the neck and then another had loomed behind it … she opened her eyes once more to regard the male before her.

He was *huge*. As huge as that shadow.

Had it been him?

She could not see how else she could have survived. In that case, he had saved her and vanquished the wight—or incapacitated it. That meant he had to be powerful—and more powerful than just his ample muscles suggested. *Magic* would be needed for such a feat. Was he elf-kind too?

Her gaze traced over him whilst he watched her steadily with storm-grey eyes that, this close, held flecks of gold woven through. His expression was impassive, one strong brow arched with the hint of a question, or perhaps concern. He had olive skin, rich and warm, and dark hair scraped into a knot at the crown of his head.

Her attention flicked to his falling hands as he dropped them into his lap and held that cloth loosely between his fingers. Giant hands. Muscled arms. Broad shoulders. A burly chest. The modest surcoat and tunic he wore barely contained him. Venya swallowed. This male was powerful in every physical sense of the word—and that was just upon the surface.

As she tentatively reached out with her magic, he inhaled and his gaze sharpened upon her. He felt her prying, even as she sensed the deep well of power in him. It was so deep she felt as though she could fall into it.

She glanced up, narrowing her eyes. He was too powerful for elfkind, at least that she had seen. She saw the taper and length of his ears. The hint of elongated, pointed canines betwixt his parted, full lips. The hint of something *other* in the bone structure of his face that was half hidden by a cropped beard that hugged his broad jawline. Registered his unnatural size anew—too big for an elf, who were more lithe of limb, finer featured, and shorter in stature.

He is faekind.

She stilled at that conclusion. All she knew of the fae were their fecund natures. Volatile. Fickle. Entirely untrustworthy.

Dangerous.

CHAPTER SEVEN

The dark sorcerer Venya sought was fae—though she doubted he would have been gracious enough to save and tend her. She swallowed.

"Who are you?" he asked, cocking his head at her.

Venya's breath shuddered, and she did not answer for a second, something private curling and tingling at the proximity of his presence, though it was not fear. This male had tended her. She had so many questions. The fae were not known as healers or for benevolence in their manners. And they were known to misuse true names. *I cannot answer that, can I?*

"Are you alright? Do you speak Common Tongue?" He arched a brow at her silence.

Her cheeks warmed. He thought her stupid. "I do," she forced out, wetting her lips. "I… What happened?"

Understanding lit his eyes. His brow softened, and he regarded her imperturbably again with those silver-and-gold eyes. She breathed in the scent of him and nearly groaned at the comfort of it. Leather and amber: warm, comforting, with a hint of exotic.

He sighed and ran a giant hand through his hair, smoothing it down. "I heard you scream. When I came upon you, you were in the barrow wight's grasp and close to death. I know not how you woke him, but you are lucky to be alive. It took all my skill to draw the death from your veins. Without help, you would have succumbed to his curse—fed that wight's power or become one yourself. The wightmark upon your neck is a light price for your encounter."

Wightmark? Venya's hand flew to her neck. It tingled under her palm, but the skin felt normal to her.

"You can see it in a mirror. Not now," he warned. "The skin is paler where it gripped you. You ought to be dead, by rights. I arrived just in time."

"You destroyed the wight."

His jaw hardened. "I did."

"Thank you," she whispered, her hands knotting together upon her chest. She gasped and sat upright. "Boy! What of B —my horse?"

Those full lips parted. A slight exhale emerged as he grimaced. "He was beyond saving."

Venya's chest caved.

"I gave him a clean end."

She could not breathe. Her head bowed over her chest. *No...* Boy had carried her faithfully for weeks now. He was feisty, yes, a little impatient for their slow pace at times but he had been her companion. Her only anchor to anything from home. And now he was gone.

"I am sorry." And the fae male did genuinely sound it. "His injury was mortal enough, but once that wight began to drain him, his soul was wight-touched. There was no return from that. Not as weak as he was."

Venya closed her eyes against the burn of tears, but they slipped free anyway. Pain brewed in her chest, but it was not the physical pain of what she had endured. The emotional guilt from Boy's death added to the tangled mess of the rest of it that sat there, fresh and waiting to gnaw at her anew. She could not breathe with the weight of it.

"Thank you," she forced out. Whatever had passed, this elf, fae, *whatever* he was, had given her steed a merciful end and ceased his suffering. Gratitude tinged her tumbling feelings towards this strange male. Whatever he was, he had been kind to her horse when he had no cause to be, and that counted in her heart for good. She was more grateful for that than that he had saved her.

"How did you defeat the wight?" she dared to voice, glancing up at him through lowered lashes.

He sat there still at the end of the bed, his hands resting in his lap, wet cloth between his fingers, at ease amongst the rumpled covers. He still watched her openly, curiously, but at her question, his expression closed.

He cocked his head. "You do not need to worry about that. Suffice to say it is not the first wight I have encountered. I guard these lands against such creatures, and purge them when necessary."

Venya swallowed. Clearly, he was not about to divulge his life story and the strength of his magic to her, a stranger on the road, but the threat in his tone was clear, and he was, it seemed, powerful enough to act upon it.

"I thank you again, then, good sir. Without you, I would not be alive." Her hand slipped to the mark on her throat. It felt strangely cool against her touch.

"It will fade in time, as you heal," he said. "You were not so badly affected—I have seen worse. It will not be permanent, perhaps."

She shivered and let her hands fall into her lap, a mirror of his, only hers wrung together.

"Do you perhaps have a horse I could borrow? I am still yet days away from my destination, I believe. I would not like to linger in these woods at the pace my own feet can sustain, if such fell creatures are the standard here." Only the guilt driving her onwards could quench her apprehension about leaving this safe space and venturing back out there where wights and possibly worse awaited.

He huffed, and one corner of his lips twitched upwards. "Perhaps, but you are foolish to journey to such parts of the world. This is the *Wildewood*. One does not simply travel here. What brings you to these parts?"

Venya swallowed. How much could she trust this stranger? This probable *fae* stranger? Her saviour or not, she would not allow it to lull her into a false sense of security. Not when she was here to find a fae sorcerer of her own, the infamous Kassimir the Dark. Was this fae his kin, perhaps? It would not do to displease him, but she could not furnish him with all of her deepest—

His voice cut into her spiralling thoughts. "Are you well?" he frowned, leaning towards her.

Her cheeks flooded red hot. "Y-yes, quite. I must be on my way, good sir."

He barked a laugh at that and raised an eyebrow, shooting her a look of derision that clearly said, *"not a chance."*

Venya struggled to pull back the coverlet, but trapped under its bulk, it was hopeless. She was still fully clad, she realised with relief, glad that this stranger had not compromised her dignity. Even though she could, with her movement, smell herself, and it was *not* so pretty as the leather and amber musk drifting from him. Oh, what she would give for a proper bath. She swallowed.

"I have to go. I cannot delay." She wrenched the cover

slightly freer and swung her leg off the bed, groaning and grimacing as a wave of pain assaulted her.

He leaned forward and planted one warm hand gently on each shoulder, but his movement was firm and unyielding as he pressed her back into the pillows.

"You're in no fit state to go anywhere," he rumbled, bending to her leg and slipping one palm behind her foot to lift it back into the bed. He tucked the coverlet in once more.

Venya gaped in indignation and shock—no one had touched her before, not like that, with such easy familiarity—and cold rushed in where a moment before, that warm, gentle touch had cupped the back of her ankle.

He sat back and folded those muscled arms across his burly chest. Ornate threads glinted at his cuffs and collar, catching the soft fire and candlelight illuminating the room.

"You need to rest—for a couple of days at the very least, perhaps more. I feel your magic healing you, and I have helped, particularly where that wightmark is concerned, but I'm afraid you require a short period of convalescence before you're fit to face the Wildewood again."

Venya shot upright. "No! I have to go! I cannot linger. My-my mother needs me," she allowed herself to admit. That did not give away any intimate secrets. "She's sick. I must find a cure for her."

The male frowned. "And you came here? You must be desperate." He pursed his lips.

"I am. She will perish if I do not return by Starfall. I cannot afford to waste time lazing about here. I'm fit enough to walk, therefore I'm fit enough to leave. I'll do anything to see her healed." *After all, it's my fault she's at death's door in the first place.*

Her breath lurched in her chest, small and pitiful next to that giant lump of guilt and the space it took up there. She had to make him understand. *Care.* Her hands scratched at her face, the burning trail of nails dragging down her cheek. That pain sharpened her. "She'll die if I don't find a cure."

"And you'll die if you venture out there in your current state."

She tried to slip her leg free, but he had trapped the duvet back in place under his own weight, and she could do little more than struggle. She let out a strangled yelp of frustration.

He laughed, rich and warm, and his eyes glittered as his lips slipped open in a wide grin, revealing those pointed canines in their entirety.

"I had you pinned for a quiet, meek mouse of an elf, but there is something fiery in you, it seems."

She glared at him indignantly. It was not the first time she had been called "mouse." That was a nickname she had hated in her teenage years, and she hated it still now for the memories it brought back.

"There's no need to be rude."

He shrugged, the roll of his shoulders nonchalant, the tug of his smirk filled with an arrogance that irritated the life out of her.

"That was a compliment."

"As backhanded a compliment as I've ever heard," she muttered, glaring at him. "Who are you, anyway? You saved me from certain death and…" Her irritation fell away as she remembered with a fresh blow to her heart. "You helped Boy, but I don't even know your name."

"And you haven't earned it," he said, tipping his chin up to regard her from beneath hooded lids. "Drink this." He pulled a vial from a pocket at his waist and held it out to her.

She glanced at him suspiciously.

"It will help." When she did not move, he added irritably, "It's your choice."

He had not hurt her so far, she reasoned. She took the vial, opened it, and downed the mouthful of contents.

"You're fae." She dared to say it. The word hung between them.

"I am."

"I'm not asking for your true name. I'm asking for you to give me anything by which to know you."

He grimaced and stood. She was forced to crane her neck back so far it hurt to look up at him from the bed.

"Perhaps. All in good time. For now—rest. You're good to no one, least of all your mother, as you are." He arched a brow, as if sensing the retort that bubbled away on her lips. "The sooner you rest, the sooner you will be."

Venya growled in frustration and slammed her head back on the pillow as he left. Exhaustion rolled over her in crashing waves. He was right. Even though she didn't want to admit it. The attack had taken more out of her than she realised—mentally, physically, and emotionally. Tears slipped from her closed eyes, sliding down her cheeks and into her hair as she mourned for Boy, until at last, she fell asleep, her handsome and mysterious fae saviour gone for now. Her questions, her fears, and her guilt would have to wait.

CHAPTER EIGHT

*K*assimir retired, brooding, to his study, taking a tumbler of fiery whisky and the bottle with him. He slumped in one of the armchairs, that tumbler held loosely in his fingers, and stared into the enchanted flames. They cast the wood-panelled, high-ceilinged room in shades of blood and amber.

His head hurt. Who was this female? She had fallen from the heavens like Arielle, the star who had done just that in the legend of Starfall, so out of place in this dark and sorcery-filled forest he could hardly understand why she had been foolish enough to venture there.

Until he had seen the desperation in her, that was. She had *clawed* at her face, leaving red furrows upon her pale cheeks, so upset was she. Pity had stirred for her. He had insisted she rest and given her a tonic that would induce a dreamless slumber for a day to help her do so, but if he were being honest with himself, it was because he hadn't decided what to do with her yet.

He had no intentions of hurting her. He was not so dastardly that he would willingly do it, and yet… He shifted in the chair and took a sip of his whisky, relishing the honey-and-oak tinged burn down his throat. And yet, her death would mean his life. That was basic self-preservation.

That her sacrifice would help bind the demon and save countless others was a more noble justification. But Kassimir was a coward. He knew it; the demon knew it. It was saving his own hide that drew him most. He owed nothing to a stranger who ought to be dead by rights, anyway.

He dragged a hand through his hair, pulling strands loose. Heavens damn him, he was a terrible soul. He could not let her leave.

"No, you cannot," that demon crooned. *"It's hopeless, but I will feed from her and enjoy the morsel, anyway. And then I will still devour you."* Ozul's invisible smile curdled dread in the pit of his belly.

Kassimir did not know whether to believe that poison. For as much as the demon had been his prisoner for so many centuries, sometimes it felt like his captor, the hold over his soul that it had, cast such a great shadow he could not hope to escape it.

"It's not hopeless," he said, but his half-hearted rebuke did not even convince him. "It's *not,*" he repeated more strongly. If he sacrificed the girl's life force at midnight on Starfall at the very moment of the curse's breaking, he could renew it. Perhaps for centuries, perhaps for decades, depending on the strength of her magic and life. But either way, he would buy more time—for himself, and for an answer.

"I shall enjoy feasting upon her and thank you for your gift, my host, but then I shall enjoy you too. You know it to be true. You feel my ascent." Ozul writhed in delight.

"My time draws near. I shall make your death deliciously slow and repay you for every second of my long imprisonment before I end you."

The tumbler slipped from Kassimir's fingers, and the delicate crystal shattered on the floor at his feet, spilling the contents across the parquet tiles and spattering his boots. Kassimir made no move, sitting with his shoulders hunched and his head bowed.

He knew what he ought to do. He ought to let the female go before she realised who he was. He should meet his fate with courage and endure his punishment—because it was no less than what he deserved. That would be what a decent male would do.

But he did not want that. He wanted to survive, even if his existence was a trapped one, a shadow of life in his self-imposed prison. He did not want to die, either, at the hands of this demon who would delight in shredding him. He wanted to *live* and if he was to preserve himself... the female had to take his place. He would have to sacrifice her himself to deliver the power needed to bind the demon anew. He feared its escape more than anything. The destruction it would wreak. How it would punish *him*.

He roared his anger at the hateful situation he found himself in, that was entirely of his own doing, and how wanting he was in moral fibre to deal with it like a fae male ought to.

Coward, damn you!

The demon repeated his own curses to him with cackles of delight. *"Coward, damn you!"* Either way, it would be fed.

Kassimir only roared all the louder, but he could not drown out the hate that was already inside him. He shot to his feet, grabbed the bottle, and launched it at the fire. It shattered on the coals and a *whoosh* boomed through the room as the spirits caught fire and quickly burned out.

CHAPTER NINE

When Venya awoke, it took her a minute to realise she was no longer in the halls of the Athenaeum, or her own bed chamber there, or in the wilds of the world. She swallowed, her mouth parched, and opened her eyes.

Stars above.

A vaulted ceiling greeted her. Eight ribs of pale stone met in a central peak above her, a star in their centre at the zenith of the room. On the soaring ceiling, exquisitely painted silver stars danced upon a canvas of blue so dark she could barely distinguish it from black.

Venya glanced around the octagonal room. Seven sides held tall windows arched to a point, stone frames carved with flowers and leaves, through which the setting sun bled light of molten gold, swathing the room in an amber glow that softened the hard stone. She saw sky and a carpet of treetops.

Am I in a tower?

The last wall held a closed iron-studded wooden door. Her gaze swept further to examine the room's contents. A wooden chest with a folded garment atop it. A small dresser with an ewer, bowl, and mirror upon it. A stool. A small bookcase with a few old volumes on it and the tell-tale dust that showed they had long been unloved. A small fire burning in a grate between two of the windows, with a flue rising into the ceiling. The bed she currently rested in was topped with soft coverlets of forest green fabrics embellished with cream embroidery.

Her fingers ran over the strangely comforting threads, but only for a moment before she pushed her aching body up to sit, and then swung her legs out of the bed, grimacing at the complaints of every muscle. She felt the magic lacing through her, healing her wounds slowly, sluggish no doubt from the exertion required.

Her thoughts waded through mud—the aches did not matter. It had been night the last she remembered. It was dusk now. She had lost at least one day, and she could not face the prospect of more. The keen edge of fear and guilt sliced through that pain, galvanising her into action.

The door clicked open. Venya froze. Yet, it was not her burly saviour that entered, but a black cat so giant and monstrous Venya froze instinctively in the face of its finger-length teeth.

The beast cocked its head at her and slipped into the room. Suddenly, the tower seemed too small. Venya felt keenly aware of her vulnerability. She glanced at her dagger in its sheath atop that chest.

Too far away.

Her magic still felt sluggish.

The beast opened its mouth. "It's dinnertime. My master is expecting you."

Venya's jaw fell. "You can speak?"

It blinked slowly at her. *"No,"* it replied, tone dripping with sarcasm.

Venya's cheeks warmed. It had not attacked her and showed no signs of predatory behaviour—the tightness in her chest eased a little. Whatever this beast was, it did not mean her any harm at that moment.

Master, it had said. Her mysterious saviour. Something stirred in the pit of her stomach.

"May I wash, first?" She could practically feel the grime crawling across her skin.

"Yes, lady. The water in the ewer is kept warm. There is a fresh garment for you on the chest. Master thought you might appreciate it." The feline glanced pointedly at her state —filthy leathers and leggings—but she could not determine any judgement in its unreadable expression.

"Thank you," she forced out. "Please give me a moment. I'll be quick."

Her stomach felt cavernously empty, gnawing at the rest of her, and her head thick with lack of water. Dinner would be good. Never had she thought she would trust to eat in the home of a fae, but the male had tended her. She was too hungry to care, perhaps, but she did not think he would go to the effort if he planned to harm her.

Relief leached the tension out of her shoulders as the beast padded away on silent paws.

Venya rushed to the ewer, clamping a hand on the wooden dresser as she reached it, for the room span around her. She closed her eyes and gritted her teeth.

Come on. Push past this.

She had to, for her mother's sake, and be on her way as soon as possible. Precious time slipped away moment by moment, like grains of sand beneath her fingers. That guilt stabbed at her anew as the memory of her mother, as she had last seen her, crashed into the forefront of her mind. A wraith in her own bed, so small that Venya could not believe how wasted away her body had become in such a brief span of time.

All your fault.

That spurred her to action. Venya stripped and poured the ewer into the bowl. Bumps rose against her skin, but it was surprisingly warm in the tower despite the ascent of winter outside, the space kept cosy by fire or magic—perhaps both. Steam rose from the water. That *had* to be magic.

Venya didn't care if it scalded. She dipped in the folded cloth next to the bowl and scrubbed at her skin furiously. Minutes later she was red raw, but she did not care. She was clean, for one. Well—*cleaner.*

She slipped into the dress, the waiting garment atop the chest, shimmying it up over her hips and settling it onto her shoulders. It was too loose and a smidge too short, but it was clean, dry, and… She inhaled deeply and breathed out an appreciative sigh. *Lemon, soap, and thyme. Far better than sweat, blood, and grime.*

There were no shoes to match the dress, though. Venya wrinkled her nose and attacked her disgusting leather boots with the same cloth, regretting how murky the water turned. However, it felt slightly better to put them on under the dress without the dirt. She glanced around. Her cloak had been folded and placed on top of the chest, next to where the dress had rested. Her belt and dagger lay upon it.

Do I dare take my dagger to dinner? Her hip felt light without the weight of it, but… *I have guest right, don't I? Do fae honour such things? Or are they barbarians?* Her host had, so far, healed her, given her shelter, and now he was about to feed her. That did not feel malevolent. Taking a dagger to dinner would most probably cause offence.

Magic tingled at her fingertips, sparked by anxiety. Well, if nothing else, she had sorcery, weak though she felt. Hesitantly, she crossed to the door. Unlocked. She opened it—and yelped.

The big cat waited outside. It stared at her in silence at the outburst.

"I'm ready," she stammered.

It turned and led the way down a narrow spiral staircase punctuated by tall arched windows that gave her a sliver of a view out over the forest to mountains in the distance.

"This way, elf." The creature turned down a long hall.

Her boots, so loud on the stone steps, were instantly muffled by long rugs that ran the length of the hall. There was a gallery of windows overlooking a walled garden, with rooms and other halls branching off. With every step, her pulse rose. Where on Altarea was she? This had not been marked on the map. Most importantly, benevolent host or not, how could she leave?

It's just dinner, she reminded herself, smoothing the front of the dress over her stomach. *Then you can sleep, and then you can leave.* She hoped. She still felt bone-achingly tired. If she had a choice, rest would be preferred by far.

"I will return you to your room after dinner." It slowed beside her.

"Thank you."

It did not reply. The feline turned down another hallway and soon after, halted at open double doors, gesturing inside. It made to leave.

Venya threw out a hand. "Wait! Do you have a name?"

It regarded her with imperturbable emerald eyes. "You may call me Pata."

"Thank you, Pata." Venya swallowed. She could not tell whether that was male, female, or neither. "I'm Venya."

Pata inclined its head and left, its paws silent across the rug. It turned the corner and vanished.

Venya's pulse notched up again, and she took a deep, shuddering breath to steady herself. Was it hot, or just her? She swallowed. No time like the present. She ran through what little she knew of the fae.

Don't give him your true name. Don't drink the wine. Fae cannot lie. Fae want to corrupt you. At the very least, she had to thank her host for his altruism despite her mistrust of his kind.

She stepped into the dining room where her saviour, the master of the house, and dangerous fae stranger awaited.

CHAPTER TEN

Venya lifted her chin under his scrutiny, openly evaluating him too. His surcoat and leathers were gone—tonight a shirt of dark fabric billowed, the sleeves rolled up to his elbows and the hem tucked into fitted leggings that emphasised the muscular form of his legs. He was the picture of informal ease and somehow, he made the vast space seem intimately full. On the long table, just two places had been set on adjacent corners before the roaring fire. He gestured to a chair.

"You will give Pata your name, but not I?" He smiled, and there was a glint of something in his eyes that flickered— mirth, or perhaps offence—before it was gone.

Venya swallowed, balling her hands into fists as she drew closer. She was not short by elven standards and yet still he towered over her, even more so as she sat in the chair and he slid it effortlessly closer to the table. So close was he, that the alluring scent of leather and amber washed over her, along with the steady comfort of a wood fire laced with pine boughs.

"Thank you."

"You're welcome, *Venya*."

She flinched and hunched her shoulders.

"Don't worry," he said, with a dark chuckle. "I shan't enchant you. Not unless you want me to."

Her cheeks flooded warm and her glare snapped to him. He only shot her a crooked smile, revealing one of those predatory canines, before slipping into the seat next to her. Their hands almost brushed as he sat.

Venya snatched her hands off the table and onto her lap. "Who are you? If you know my name, I must have one from you."

A name and more besides. What was this wondrous place in the middle of nowhere—in the middle of a forsaken place like the Wildewood, no less? Maps did not chart such areas, but she had never thought to find anyone living here willingly or in anything but squalor and danger. Only an exiled sorcerer who had no other choice.

He did not reply, only glanced at her lazily. "Wine?"

She shook her head.

He frowned. "It's not fae wine, if you are concerned. I do not partake."

"Water is fine." She did not drink either—not since a particularly terrible morning after a ghastly night long ago that she tried not to remember.

"Water it is." He picked up a jug—tiny in his giant grasp—and filled the ornate fluted glass before her.

"Thank you," she said, her manners automatic. "And your name?" She arched a brow.

He laughed, rich and deep. "You do not want that."

"I don't want your true name, if you are concerned." She flipped his words back upon him.

He shot her a glare filled with such wicked mischief and delight that it made something within her tighten. This close, those steel eyes with their gold flecks were impossible to look away from.

Venya wrenched her glare aside. *Do not fall for his fae wiles.*

She was not there for the fun of daydreaming, and nothing more than that would be possible. Not for the likes of her. She had long ago concluded that she was too plain and too unusual to be desired. And when anyone did draw close, the moment they discovered her family name—Ravakian, cursed with the treachery of her ancestors—that was enough to seal the nail in the coffin of any promise. Her grimoires were her companions; the magical and feisty tomes that she tended for a living. They did not judge her. She felt bare without them, and utterly alone.

"Where did you go?" he asked, his voice so surprisingly soft that it was that unexpected tone which jolted her from her reverie. "You disappeared somewhere deep just then."

"I apologise," she said stiffly, straightening her back against the hard chair. Her eyes dropped to the silverware on the table.

He regarded her for a second before realising she was not about to explain herself to him. "Dinner then. Let us eat." His tone was light, his rich voice rumbling through her, warm and inviting. "You must be famished."

"Please. How long have I been here?" She shot him a pleading glance.

His frown softened. "Two days. You needed the rest."

Venya's eyes slipped shut. She forced them open. Two days lost from an already impossibly short timeline. Now, she had even less time to find a cure for her mother and return home. Anxiety poisoned the hunger gnawing at her belly to a sick dread that roiled.

Her rescuer turned his palms face up on the table, splaying his fingers, and drew in a breath. She felt the rush of magic pass through her, its wild power heady and intoxicating.

Food materialised on the table before them, filling the surface closest to them with all manner of dishes. Rich, meaty scents laced with herbs and the sharp tang of fruit smothered his leather and musk.

Venya's mouth fell open. *How did he do that?* She ought to have been scared at the casual display of power, perhaps, but it was fascinating.

He began spooning food onto her empty plate. Herby potatoes. Cuts of succulent meat still pink in the middle. Vegetables cooked in butter and mixed with nuts and berries. A ladle of rich gravy to blanket it all.

Her tongue *hurt*, the smell of it was so tangibly rich and thick.

"Eat. Please," he invited, waiting for her to pick up her cutlery before he too joined her. For all that he was fae, she had not expected him to be so civilised.

There was silence as Venya ate and drank—with as much decorum as she could manage in her half-starved state—and then, her plate was empty, his too. Then the plundered platters and their used plates disappeared into nothing with another rush of magic.

"Better?" He raised an eyebrow, cocking his head and looking at her in a way that felt strangely intimate.

"Yes." Emboldened, she continued, "I must have your name. Come. It seems so strange that you have something to call me, and yet I know nothing of you."

He paused, his mouth ajar.

"No?" Venya huffed. "Fine. I shall name you myself. I shall call you..." she fished for a name. So close to Starfall, with the draw of its date guiding her so strongly in her mission, for Starfall was her deadline to return home, there was only one that came to mind. "Leander."

He recoiled and regarded her with a strange frown and a half smile. "Leander? From the fairy-tale?"

She laughed, a delighted peal that sprang forth unbidden. "Yes! You know of it?" This fae male only grew stranger and more unexpected.

"Of course. Who does not know the tale of those two star-crossed lovers?" He leaned forward on the table, propping up his chin on joined fists.

He was so close, his gaze locking onto hers, that her breath caught.

"I am no mortal," he said.

"I know. But if you will give me no other name, then I shall name you myself. If you give me more time, Leander, perhaps I can think of a more fitting choice."

He huffed. "I should think so. I ought to at the very least be an Aleksandor, or perhaps a Baern."

She snorted. "Aleksandor? *Baern?*" Two legends of fae and elfkind, respectively. Was she more surprised that he was well read enough to know of them, or that his ego was big enough to compare himself with them?

"Yes!" he said indignantly, brows plunging together. He sat back and folded his arms in a motion so distinctly childlike it reminded her of her brother sulking as a child.

She could not stifle the giggle that slipped out.

"Unbelievable," he muttered.

"I do not mean to be rude, good sir, for I appreciate your protection and hospitality. However, I'll stick with *Leander*. Perhaps then you might be persuaded to give me your real name."

"So devious, little mouse." His stare turned daring. "Perhaps I should call you Arielle."

Heat flared inside her. She pushed her chair back. "You

already have my name, though I did not give it to you. I ought to retire, for I must be away early tomorrow."

He pursed his lips and his frown soured. "You require at least three more days to recover, if not longer. The wight-mark still lingers upon your neck. The malice of its magic must be gone ere you venture from here. Like calls to like; dark to dark, light to light… death to death. I would not wish you to draw anything untoward upon the road."

At that thought, at the memory it brought forth of death and fear, she shuddered.

He stood and offered her a hand to stand. "Enough of that," he said, as though he had perceived where her mind wandered. "Come. It is rare that I have guests. Let me show you around this home of mine. If you like stories, you shall enjoy my library."

A library. Her heart flipped. Her whole life revolved around books—she was a librarian at Pelenor's finest and largest Athenaeum, keeper of the magical grimoires there. She always had time for books. She nodded and smiled, a true smile that he instinctively matched.

"That would be amenable."

Venya slipped her fingers into his palm, suppressing a hiss with the way his warm hand closed around hers. It was all too pleasant. He drew her to her feet and hooked her hand into the crook of his burly arm. They were so close, her breath hitched. She felt the heat radiating from him, and once more that warm, alluring scent of his enveloped her.

She had avoided the fae wine, and she had sensed no enchantment upon her food, but fae were masters of other wiles too, more base and tempting. *This is a daydream. A distraction. He is handsome and kind, nothing more,* she reminded herself. *Anything else is nothing but fae wiles and charm.*

Would that be so bad? a small voice inside wheedled. She stamped on it. Hard. She had no time for distractions. And besides, she did not deserve such a pleasant pastime, even if she had an opportunity for it.

Venya raised her chin and followed his lead from the dining hall. A handsome face and unexpected opportunity would not distract her from a mission of life and death. No matter his argument, she had to leave. Sooner rather than later. Her mother—and her own conscience—depended on it. If she failed, Venya would never forgive herself.

CHAPTER ELEVEN

*H*er hand was so small in the crook of Kass's arm, as though she were a ghost that would slip away at any second. Kass had his fair share of those haunting his halls and usually he longed for nothing more than to escape them.

Yet, she was so *real*. So warm and full of life. Those violet eyes of hers enchanted him, a window into her soul. He had no intention of wasting a minute of her company, pleasant as she was and so starved of it was he.

He led her down the long gallery and past the secure library—he would show it to her another time, perhaps. She had faced down a wight, but how would she feel about the wild grimoires he created when the whim took him? They could be violent and odious little malevolences when they wished. That would be a supervised visit. He had no intention of letting her wander in there unaccompanied and stumbling upon trouble.

"I shall show you the library tomorrow," he promised as he had to tug her past. She had paused, her eyes filled with such yearning, her body turning towards that doorway, and it sparked something within him. He smiled at the small groan that escaped her. "It is magnificent in the daytime when the sun streams in." *If* the sun streamed in. Those days were few and far between in winter.

"Here. Let us retire to the drawing room." It felt so strange to roll so many words around his tongue. He had grown so used to being short and economical when it came to speaking with Pata or any of the other creatures or grimoires he called companions. His mouth practically ached from it.

She slipped her hand free of his elbow at last. He held the door open for her, guiding her with a gentle touch on the small of her back to one of the high, wingback armchairs circled intimately before the fire. A blaze sprung to life at a wave of his hand, bathing the room in instant warmth and light.

"Oh!" she exclaimed and veered away from him towards the bookshelves lining one of the walls. She busied herself in the shelves immediately, flitting to and fro. He watched her, his head cocked. A smile ghosted his lips as he saw the obvious care and pleasure she took from examining this small part of his collection—mainly historical and philo-sophical titles and most of them rare volumes—with obvious appreciation and awe.

As she stroked spines, pulled out a volume here and there to glance at the front or back matter and flick through them, before sliding them carefully back into their well-crafted spaces, something inside him could not help but stir. At the knit of her brows and wide wonder of her eyes, flummoxed and awed by what she delved into. At the complete ignorance of him, so absorbed in her pursuit. At the twig stuck in the end of her braid— She had not had a chance to bathe prop-erly yet, after all, and he would not mention it for fear of embarrassing her. He felt the fragility of her ego almost viscerally. She would mistake the kindness of its mention for shaming.

He was attracted to her—and somehow, she seemed to fit there, moving between his books. In his space. Her sweet lemon and lavender scent mixed with leather and earth from the road. He gripped the back of one of those armchairs as the fancy took him. How nice it would be to have someone to share this place with besides sentient grimoires and magical beasts of his own creation. It had felt like a lifetime, and he yearned for the company.

He did not deserve any of that happy vision. He swallowed. Why was there a hard lump in his throat?

"You like to read?" He cleared his throat around his hoarse voice and pushed away from the chair, clasping his arms behind his back as he sauntered across to her, attempting to appear the very picture of calm.

She glanced at him at last, life sparkling in her eyes, one of his books held open loosely in her hands. "You could say that. I am a librarian. I collect and manage grimoires for the Royal Athenaeum of Pelenor."

He chuckled. "Perhaps I ought to have guessed that. You are more interested in these than anything else." He gestured to the shelves. *Grimoires, eh?*

Instantly, she flooded red, and her knuckles whitened as her grip tightened on the book. "I didn't mean to be rude."

"Not at all." He gestured to the book in her hands. "A beautiful account of old Aegillian history. I could translate for you, if you need?"

Her smile was small, no arrogance in it as she said, "I am fluent."

His brow arched. "In a dead tongue?"

"It's only dead if no one speaks it."

"Hmm. By definition, it is dead if there are no natives left to voice it."

That book closed, and she pulled it against her stomach, circling her arms around it almost protectively. "I know that is the true definition, but don't you find that so sad? That's why I like to think of it this way. That such tongues are not dead—nor the memory of their rich peoples—unless they are forever lost to the dust of time."

"Well, then." He stepped closer and eased the tome from her arms. "Perhaps you can read it to me. I would deeply enjoy you bringing life to ancient Aegillian once more."

She coloured, dropped her gaze, and shrunk away.

Is she so shy? He frowned. He was not used to dealing with such fragility. "Or not. It is of no matter." He offered her the book, and she slipped it back onto the shelf, then brushed past him to stand at the tall window.

It was dark and moonless outside—the glass appeared black behind her, silhouetting her slender, willowy form against it. He longed to cross the space to her. She intrigued him so, strange creature that she was. Filled with such passion and yet such restraint that it all but quashed the life in her whenever she realised it had slipped free.

She would hate him truly if she knew who he really was. For one, he did not collect, protect, and contain grimoires like her. In Pelenor, what he did was forbidden. He *made* grimoires.

CHAPTER TWELVE

This haven inside the Wildewood delighted Venya. It held everything she enjoyed—and in that was its greatest, alluring danger. Her finger traced the carved stone windowsill as she looked out into the night sky from the drawing room. She saw little now, illuminated as the room was by candlelight and fire. Outside, the shy moon had wreathed itself in molten silver clouds.

The place stood in astounding contrast to the threatening forest she had entered mere days before. Beautiful architecture, carefully wrought by craftsmen long dead. Gardens that she estimated would be blooming and beautiful come the spring and summer. A library to rival the personal collection of her family, she reckoned—for that alone, she would have stayed, had need not driven her. Food so luscious her tongue had never been treated to such fine fare that delighted with every mouthful. Warmth and comfort, despite the size of the place—not once yet had she felt the draught or chill that seemed inevitable in such places.

Beyond those gardens, beautiful mountains ringed the horizon with snow-capped peaks and circled the wide skies giving a perfect view of the constellations high above on clear nights. And, though she did not want to admit it to herself, a host that, through his enigmatic attitude, alluring appearance, and unfailing generosity, softened her protective shell more than she wanted.

Oh yes. This was a place she could happily stay for a day, a month, a year—or perhaps longer. Everything seemed so perfect. An idyllic retreat from the painful reality of her life. She needed to press on, but her soul cried out to rest here. With him. Her host seemed so charming and genuine, and though it was dangerously foolish, a part of her daydreamed about being freed of the confines of her life to enjoy a moment instead if she dared.

What she sought would not be so fine as this place. She pictured miserable, cold, wet mountains. Perhaps a dank-half ruin. A cruel fae sorcerer. Venya shivered and wrapped the coverlet tighter. The warmth of the fire, the inherent cosiness of the place, struggled to break through the cold dread that still circled inside her.

No doubt, she would have to bargain a painful price to obtain what she so desperately needed. She would do it. A thousand times over. Even give her soul, if she had to, to secure a cure for her mother.

"You do not have to rush back out there, you know." He appeared at her side, a solid, reassuring presence that tempted her to turn towards it.

Her hands grasped the stone sill, the grain of it biting into her fingertips.

"I must."

He angled towards her, the deep shadows making his frown more severe. "What is so urgent that you would willingly do so? It is not a place one ought to wonder. There are dangerous beasts around, and more, as you well know."

Venya swallowed around the budding lump in her throat. "It is not a case of desire. I *have* to. My mother. She sickens. It's my fault, and I'm responsible for finding a cure."

"Your fault?" he interrupted, raising a brow. "I find that hard to believe."

"It is." She closed her eyes and rested her forehead against the cold glass. "There were complications when I was born. My twin brother was birthed easily. And I? Not so." Her voice had fallen to a whisper now. Admitting this felt too painful. Too shameful. Even to a stranger. He would judge her harshly, but it was no more than she deserved.

"I-I got stuck, and they couldn't free me. It was a long and complex labour. In the end, we were both saved, by what grace I do not know, but Mother almost died. She has suffered heart troubles since. The healers worked their magic on her to the extent of their abilities. She receives regular treatment—she has done all my life—but always with the full knowledge that one day, those treatments would become less and less effective. One day, they would fail. And one day, her heart would give out."

She pulled away from the glass and folded her arms around herself, hunching her shoulders over. Skies above, that shard of pain was too much to bear at times, so sharp she could not breathe. It was so laced with guilt that every beat of her own heart felt like a curse, not a blessing, a reminder of the punishment she deserved.

"You blame yourself for that?" He sounded angry. He had every right to be.

"Yes. It was my fault. If I had just delivered easier, sooner, quicker, she wouldn't be on her deathbed now."

"That's ridiculous," he said hotly, and with her glance cast down, she saw his hands ball into fists. "That wasn't your fault."

Her gaze snapped up. "W-wh… I beg your pardon?" She caught herself.

He bent towards her and she retreated, her back to the wall beside the window. Cold seeped through the back of her dress. He placed a hand on the stone to either side of her head and leaned closer. So close that their lips were a span apart, their brows threatening to touch. So close that those gold-and-silver eyes swallowed her whole. So close his hot breath caressed her lips.

Something tightened, her senses on full alert at his proximity, and at those *fangs*.

"That was not your fault," he repeated, grinding it out through a clenched jaw. "When you said you were responsible, I thought you had done something terrible. Cursed her. *Injured* her. This? This is the most inane self-flagellation I have ever seen. You are not responsible that your mother chose to birth you. She knew the risks. She undertook them. That was nothing to do with you. This is all on *her*." He retreated, his hands falling away.

"How can you say that?" she gasped. His words were so cruel, each one fell like a blow, even though they were not aimed at her. "No, you don't understand, this is, I mean, I just need to find a cure."

He opened his mouth as if to retort, but she cut him off and stepped forward, her hands finding their way to his chest and clenching into fists in the billowing shirt, her whole body desperate to make him understand.

"*Please*. I have tried *everything*. Regardless of whether you blame me or not, I have tried everything. We all have. I sought every healer, academic, and text I could. I travelled to every athenaeum and library and infirmary on the continent. I sent word to any I could not reach beyond the seas. There's only one more avenue left to try, and that's why I'm here.

You have to help me. I know you owe me nothing—but she will die if I do not succeed. I'm *begging* you."

Surprise stabbed through him, widening his eyes, and he eased back a touch, those full lips parting but no words tumbling forth. Venya gasped and dropped her hands, stepping back against the cold stone, her cheeks burning with the impropriety of her actions.

"I'm s-sorry," she stammered. "I didn't mean to." She smoothed his now-creased shirt with shaking hands and then snatched them away again, wrapping her arms across her stomach.

"No apology needed," he growled.

Was that anger or something else flickering in his eyes? She could not tell. An edge of fear needled through her. Incredible though this place was, alluring though *he* was, she had to remember. He was fae. This was the Wildewood. She could not afford to let her guard down.

"Please, help me," she said again, staring up at him, trying to convey just how desperate she was with those three simple words. "I have to find Kassimir the Dark and obtain a cure for my mother."

A reflexive laugh almost burst from him, only stayed by shock. *Kassimir the Dark*, she had said. She had come for… him?

The sheer irony of it was not lost upon him—that she had sought him so desperately, that she had found him, and that she yet had no inkling.

Kass wheeled away and stormed to the fireplace, resting a hand on the mantel.

She followed. "Please. I know it's unorthodox, but I have tried everything I can, and his dark sorcery may be the only answer."

He cast a baleful look her way. "You do not know what you ask for."

"I will do anything to save her."

Kass sighed and ran a hand across his hair. *It is as though the stars truly answered my prayers. Right when I needed someone, she appeared. A gift from the heavens.*

It was not as easy as that. She watched him, her wide eyes anxious and glistening with unshed tears. Even in such distress, she was beautiful—inside and out. She had a good soul. Unlike him. Someone like her… She felt like a balm and he craved that for his own pain, selfish though it was. Every second that stretched tore his guilt into new ribbons that further tangled him up.

The demon writhed with glee inside him. Venya did not know who he was, but she would soon enough. He could not outrun the truth forever.

His voice was thick when he answered, "I will help you if I can." Truth be told, he did not know if he could—but he could not add to her distress.

SHE FELT like a fool for baring her heart so easily to a stranger, and yet once again, he had been so kind. She sensed he had tried to distract her from her upset because they had spent the next hour seated on adjacent sofas in the drawing room—him with a leg curled underneath him in a reassuringly informal manner, leaning close over the sofa arm as he showed her some of the more interesting and rare texts from that part of his collection.

It raised her mood incomparably—she could not help but be fascinated by the wealth of this fae's books. It was impossible to resist the appeal of a well-travelled, well-educated individual—and his kindness. It was far from the indifference of animosity she was used to as a bearer of the Ravakian name. That coloured so much of people's opinions of her before they had ever given her a chance to prove herself.

Here, the pleasure lay in such freeing anonymity. It did not matter who either of them was, not really. She revelled in being able to take him at face value, knowing he did the same with her. Her soul rather craved the kindness.

She glanced up to catch him smiling ever so slightly at

her. His expression blanked, and he straightened, clearing his throat, as he realised she watched him. Her cheeks warmed.

"One more, I think, and then we both ought to retire," he said, pushing to his feet. "I have a special one. Wait a moment." He crossed the room to an ornate wooden desk in the corner beside a tall window that Venya reckoned would give the most incredible mountain views come daytime and rummaged in a drawer. His hands were carefully slow as he lifted a small book out.

He returned to her side, and this time sat beside her.

Venya hissed a sharp intake of breath at his proximity. Warmth poured from him—she felt the heat of his thigh almost touching hers.

"Here." He held out the little book to her.

She took it, their fingers brushing—his were rough and slightly calloused. "A Tale of Starfall," she whispered. The title was in another language—an old tongue, but one she knew. Venya looked up at him, a question in her eyes.

He smiled, open and warm, as he nodded. "This is an original from Sainira. Since you named me Leander, I thought you might like it."

Her voice was hushed as she replied, "I cannot touch this. Do you have gloves? This is too precious to handle. The oils from my skin—"

"I have laid protective wards on every page. It is no concern."

A moan of pleasure escaped her as she ran a finger over the book cover, slightly rough, and turned to the first page. Smooth. And that smell... She breathed it deeply. This was old indeed. She slowly turned through the book, admiring the handwritten tale painstakingly lettered, with illuminated headers and twining borders of vines and stars. She reached the final page, upon which was illustrated a picture of

Leander himself, prone upon the ground with his head in Arielle's lap as she looked to the skies.

Once upon a time, she had translated this for entertainment when she had taught herself this tongue. Stroking the cover brought back a haze of memories of sun-soaked days in her dormitory as a younger trainee librarian.

"Thank you for sharing this with me. I have not seen a copy this old before." She handed it back, somewhat reluctantly.

"It seems it is a tale that transcends many cultures." He rose to return it to his desk drawer.

"And why would it not? A tale of true love that crossed an immeasurable gulf. A tragedy wrought upon the stars themselves."

He furrowed a brow at that. "I prefer to think of it as a redemption. Leander was a mortal for all his failings, and yet, he was still worthy of Arielle."

Venya smiled. "So, you are a hopeless romantic then, Leander."

His attention snapped to her, and his reply was hot. "I am not."

"I think the gentleman doth protest too much," she dared to say.

He snorted. "I am no gentleman. I merely…" He faltered.

She tilted her head, watching him. That silence between them felt altogether too fragile all of a sudden.

"It gives me hope that no one is beyond redemption." Something ticked in his clenched jaw and he shut the drawer roughly.

"I did not mean to offend you."

His jaw softened. "You did not. Come. It is late and you ought to rest."

He crossed to her and offered his hand to help her stand.

She took it—she did not need his help, but for once, it was simply nice to enjoy this meaningless connection between them. She longed for it to be real, for all her worldly cares to be stripped away, for the peace of that evening had been so soothing on her fractured and aching heart, burdened as she was with her cause. She wished she could indulge in it for days or weeks more.

They walked together in silence, arms almost brushing, down the hallways until they had reached the stairs leading up to her tower room.

He bowed to her. "Sleep well." He lingered a moment, something unreadable in his gaze, before he retreated with quiet footsteps down the hallway.

Venya slipped up the stairs to her room, her heart lighter than it had been in years.

CHAPTER FOURTEEN

Kass watched her over the breakfast table. Her breakfast—fresh pasties and fruits—lay half eaten and forgotten. Instead, she stared out of the tall windows. Last night they had been black. In the day, the mountains were visible ringing the valley, their tops shrouded by snowstorms. It cast a flat light over the valley, but she seemed fascinated by it.

Pata sidled around the door.

"Yes?" he said.

She started at that, and her attention followed his.

"Do as you wish. I have no need of you today," Kass said. "I shall look after our guest."

Her cheeks flushed at that, a pleasantly rosy pallor bringing a warm contrast to her dark hair. She dropped her attention to her plate.

"So, Venya," he said, rolling her name around his tongue. "Indulge my loneliness. Come. Tell me where you are from."

She swallowed her mouthful and took a sip of juice. "I hail from Pelenor—all of my family does. As I said, I'm a librarian at the Royal Athenaeum. My life is books, books, and more books. I curate the grimoire collections—containment, cataloguing, maintenance, research and the like. I used to work there all the time. Now, I travel sometimes to collect rare specimens."

Grimoires. His interest was piqued. She really was an unusual specimen. "And you like that?"

She shot him a look. "Of course. Books—grimoires—I rather prefer to my own kind, most of the time." She flushed red as he laughed.

"I feel much the same."

"What is your name? Your proper name? Do not worry, I do not mean your *true* name. Likely you do not even know that yet." Such things could take a lifetime to divine. "I mean the name your parents bestowed upon you."

She frowned at him. He saw her evaluating whether to answer. He kept his expression placid. Affable.

"Venya Rowena Bettany of House Ravakian."

He arched a brow. "House Ravakian," Kass repeated slowly, the syllables like water rippling off his tongue. He did not miss the way her entire being closed. Her face turned thunderous, her body pulling in on itself. Breakfast, once more forgotten. He had heard of the Ravakian name, well-read and travelled as he was. He had passed through Pelenor fleetingly, centuries back.

Ravakian… a name of evil, if one traced back far enough. This young woman bore no darkness in her—he ought to know—the like inside his soul of that cursed demon would call to hers if she possessed such shadows.

"Why are you ashamed?" Her anguish cut into him. It intensified his own guilt. Perhaps he ought to be pleased. If any name deserved no mercy, it would be hers, and yet, he could not steel his heart in her presence. It melted instead.

Her gaze flashed to his, but she did not answer.

"You have no cause to be. Your ancestors were ambitious. That is a quality I admire. They failed—not so good, perhaps. Their ambitions were less than noble; perhaps that is the difference." He shrugged. "That has nothing to do with you."

Nevertheless, it would not change what he had to do. He would feel every ounce of what he did to her in the end, though it would make him irredeemably wretched.

He broke a roll of bread and slathered it with honey fresh from the comb, deliberately turning his scrutiny from her, and trying not to turn inwards upon his own roiling feelings. Focusing instead on the smooth glide of that knife and the surging tide of golden honey chasing across the slice of bread.

As expected, her posture eased and after a moment, she nodded and resumed eating, but did not speak again.

Ravakian, he mused. Evidently, it was a legacy she did not wish for. Understandable, perhaps. None of the tales he had heard connected to the Ravakian name were positive.

"I have given you my name," she said at last. "It is only fair you give me yours. I cannot call you Leander forever."

Kass's lips thinned. He placed his knife on the plate with a soft chink. What was the use of hiding it? She would know in the end. He already knew he could not let her leave. She may as well know as much of the truth as he could give her. He owed her that much.

"Fine." He steeled himself and met her gaze. She looked at him, still with furrowed brows, her violet eyes dark in the dim winter light.

"I am Kassimir de Rochefort—or as you would call me," —his mouth took on a sneer— "Kassimir the Dark."

CHAPTER FIFTEEN

Silence lingered for a moment. Then Venya shoved back her chair, the legs screeching on the stone floor, and shot to her feet.

"No, you're not."

He only stared at her impassively. Even with him seated, she barely had to look down at him.

"You're not," she repeated. "You can't be." This time, less certain.

Still, he watched her.

"Y-you…" She could not reconcile it. This fae male had been so generous to her. Saving her from certain death at the hands of the barrow wight. Healing her. Giving her guest right. More than that, connecting with her, sharing his books, poring over that precious old edition of *A Tale of Star-fall* together, feeding her, seeming to enjoy her company…

She wanted to vomit. She wheeled around and marched to the window, desperate for fresh air. The skirts of today's dress felt too constraining around her ankles. She longed for her breeches and boots, but they had vanished and had not returned.

As she unlatched the window, a cold blast stayed her roiling stomach. *Have I been a fool?* Of course, she had come to the Wildewood to find herself a fae sorcerer. She had not expected *this*. But how many fae males would be ensconced in the midst of that forsaken forest? She groaned and closed her eyes, shutting out the vista through the glass.

How could he be Kassimir the Dark? And… how could he *not*? No one would lie about such a wicked thing. She turned to her host and evaluated him with fresh eyes. Here he was in the flesh. The Devastator of Laurent, the Soul of Darkness, the Darkyn Wielder, Terror of the Twilight.

And yet, all the terrible names she had heard of him did not add up at all to the male who had tended her through a grievous injury with soft hands, respect, and kindness.

Her hand flew to her throat. That cold wightmark was still stark upon her skin and cool to the touch, though she thought it had faded ever so slightly. Had he enchanted her to trust him? Perhaps this was a glamour. Perhaps she was in the ruinous keep she had expected all along, charmed to appear comfortable and homely. She sank back onto the windowsill, her hands clutching the stone, the rough grain biting into her palms. This felt so real.

He still watched her, evaluating her reaction with an impassive expression, but as he watched her, his face closed.

Venya swallowed. She had no choice. "You are truly Kassimir the Dark?"

He clenched his jaw. "I prefer Kassimir de Rochefort, but yes."

She steeled herself and stepped towards him, before sinking into a bow—she was hopeless at curtseys. "In that case, sir, I thank you for your hospitality and your kindness. It seems I do not need to travel any further."

She stepped closer still, now half a dozen feet away, and

dropped to one knee, staring up at him and holding herself firm. "I beg you for a cure for my mother. I will do *anything* you ask of me. I cannot leave without your aid."

Her heart hammered in her chest and her fists—one clenched by her side, one clenched across her knee—were sweaty and shaking. What terrible thing would he ask of her? She forced herself to keep her eyes open, to keep meeting his gaze, refusing to cower before him. Her mother depended on this very moment.

CHAPTER SIXTEEN

*Y*ou *cannot leave at all, though you do not know it yet.* Heavens above, he was despicable. His hard heart melted at her open prostration—how could it not—no matter how hard he tried to harden it.

Could I heal her mother? Fae magic was entirely different from elven magic. More powerful, for one. More free, wild, and potent.

"Stand up," he said. He could spare no more words. That irritating lump in his throat had returned, curse his weakness. Had he truly been alone for so long that he softened in the face of such things?

She rose in silence. He felt the weight of her unrelenting attention upon him. He beckoned her closer. She drifted towards him. He saw how reluctant she was to draw near—such a contrast. The previous night, they had been practically conjoined in his drawing room.

"If I may. Let me see into your mind—only what you wish— of your mother, so that I may understand her condition better."

She swallowed, nodded, and offered her hand to him.

He did not need it, for he could bridge the mental gap between them easily enough, but it would help strengthen the power of his scrying into her mind. He took her hand, clasping it between his calloused palms.

"Close your eyes," he said softly. She did so. He did not need that either, but he could not bear her judgement a second longer.

He closed his too, and sunk into the recesses of his mind, using the feel of her smooth skin upon his as a bridge between them. Into her mind, he slipped. He frowned against the weight of grief and guilt and shame and fear that engulfed him. Was this how she lived every day? He felt as though he could barely stagger through it. He carried just as heavy a burden, but at least his was deserved. That she carried this made him grieve for her. This was not her fault. Not her responsibility. And yet, she carried it as though it were both.

He sought memories of her mother and she pushed them to him willingly. Venya's life flashed through his mind in snippets from youth to present, all those windows into her mother's life and health. He saw everything she had done, how desperately she had tried to find a cure for what she perceived was her own fault. To no avail.

In those moments, she was vulnerable and utterly at his mercy, more than anyone who had stood before him for hundreds of years—and willingly so. She had no idea what he was capable of. What he would do to her.

It terrified him. He could not face it. She had heard about his terrible reputation, but she did not *know*. Had not seen it for herself. Thrown off, his throat closed.

Kass dropped her hand as though it had burned him. Her eyes flicked open.

He could not like her. Could not soften to her. Could not do the right thing. It would be the damned death of him.

"No," he growled, standing so quickly she fell back, fear flashing through her at his guttural tone. Kass stormed out, leaving her silent in his wake.

CHAPTER SEVENTEEN

*V*enya sprinted back to her room, taking the twists and turns at speed. Any sense of security was utterly false. Her room was no safer than anywhere else in the damned place if this was indeed Kassimir the Dark's abode, but it was the closest thing to a sanctuary she had. At least she could barricade the door.

Barricade it, she did, dropping the wooden bar across it. It wouldn't stop him if he wanted, but all the same, she needed the feeling of safety and retreat. She paced around the room, her head spinning and with a fresh fear lining her belly.

She was inside the home of the very enemy she had sought all along, the monster that was Kassimir the Dark. She was uncertain if that was what scared her the most. No. What truly terrified her was that, if she were being truthful, he was not the monster she had expected. That complicated *everything*.

She stalled at the sight of the white sky outside. Blizzards marched down the mountains, and flurries of snow danced on the breeze outside. At the very least, they would make the roads harder to travel. She had mere weeks left. Starfall approached. She *had* to be home by Starfall if her mother was to stand a chance. Venya reckoned she had a few days left before she would have to make the return journey to stand any chance of seeing her mother again.

Venya groaned and sunk onto her bed, her face falling into her hands. *I've been so stupid. So blind.* She had been duped—nearly duped—by Kassimir the Dark himself. She had considered him likeable. Attractive. Alluring. Now she knew the truth. She could not lower her guard like that again. Whatever happened next, Venya had to keep her wits about her.

You have to obtain a cure. No matter the cost. And soon.

CHAPTER EIGHTEEN

"Go away." Kass did not want to speak to anyone. He lay face down on his bed, head stuffed into the pillow.

Pata entered his chamber anyway, staring at him reproachfully.

Kass groaned. "What do you want?"

"You're being exceptionally rude, Kass. What did the girl do to earn it? Nothing, I estimate."

Kass shot the panther a venomous glare and lobbed the pillow at him.

Pata dodged it and yowled angrily at him. "Don't you start."

"Aren't I supposed to be your master?" Kass grumbled.

"Not when you act like an ogre. Go out there and make it right. You scared her. She spent the whole day barricaded in the tower and she won't come to dinner. She's on the gallery now. I persuaded her to emerge for some fresh air. You're welcome."

Kass groaned.

"You need to make this right."

But I can't. I can only make this so much worse. And damn it, he despised himself even more for it.

"Fine." Kass sighed. He could heal her mother. He had the sorcery to be able to reinforce her heart, ensure it would never trouble her the rest of her long life, but if he gave Venya that cure, she would leave.

Kass *had* to make her stay. He did not want to force her, coward though he was, for he knew he would have to force her in the end. She would not go to her own end willingly, if she knew what he had to do. What he had to do, but did not want to. What he had to do, and saw no way out of.

He ground his teeth.

"She will be a lamb to slaughter, only realising the moment the blade bites, and I shall revel in the power of her terror," goaded the demon. He did not have the will to contain Ozul. It was true, after all. He deserved to feel all the pain she would feel.

"Kass?" Pata was still there.

Kass opened an eye. The panther waited.

"Alright. I'm going."

KASS FOUND Venya on the gallery, a sheltered bridge that linked two parts of the building. It was freezing, a snowstorm was approaching. Her cloak was too thin to protect her.

She turned to him, shivering, her arms folded. Her eyes were puffy and red. He cursed himself all over again.

"I apologise for not being forthcoming with my identity," he forced himself to say. "I do not like to share it."

"I understand," she replied, but her body was closed, her face hard.

Perhaps she did understand, to an extent, being a Ravakian.

"I beg you once again." He saw how she forced herself to raise her shoulders, tip her chin up, and stare at him with such burning intensity. "*Please*. Please help me cure my mother. I will do anything."

"I have a proposal for you."

She remained silent, but her lips parted.

His stomach lurched, nausea roiling. Why was this so difficult? "I can cure your mother. For life."

Her lips parted, her chest rose with a giant intake of breath, and her face lit up with fresh hope, any animosity between them vanishing in an instant. It made his heart ache.

He licked his lips. "I will make it so, if you do one thing."

"Anything." Her answer was instant.

"Marry me. On Starfall."

Her expression froze—and then fell. She did not answer.

"Become my bride," he said. Perhaps he had stammered or stumbled. His pulse thundered so loud in his ears he heard nothing but roaring.

Still, she stared at him in utter shock.

It was a desperate attempt, the foolish romantic in him hopeful. It had saved Arielle and Leander, after all. They had ascended to the heavens together—and it was fae tradition that any union on Starfall since would be heaven-blessed. Their stars danced even now in the courts above.

If she agreed to stay, he could buy himself time to find a better answer than to sacrifice her whilst she willingly remained, content in the knowledge that he had at least answered her most pressing grief and guilt-stricken quest. It would not redeem him, but at least others would benefit from her sacrifice too, not just those in the vicinity of the

Wildewood and beyond, that the demon would have so glee-fully slain upon its release.

"*It won't work…*" said the demon lazily.

Oh, cease and be gone, you wretch! he implored it.

A chuckle answered him.

CHAPTER NINETEEN

Venya could not leave without Kassimir's grace, or a cure for her mother. She had resolved to persuade him to help, no matter the cost, and begged him again, staring into those hard-to-resist gold-flecked silver eyes… but the soft bow of his lips had just uttered unthinkable words, carried to her on that slight winter breeze.

Marry me on Starfall. Become my bride.

She assumed she had misheard at first, but as the silence yawned between them, and his expectations, she realised with a cold curl deep in her belly, one of pure fear, that she was not mistaken at all.

She had offered him *anything*. Without thinking of the ramifications, the possibilities—the reality of what he would request.

Her.

"No," she blurted at last. The bridge creaked in the wind as though the very place objected too.

That can't happen. Ever.

Venya did not suffer relationships. She had resisted an arranged marriage for convenience or class, as was customary in the old noble families like hers. She was entirely unsuitable for marriage. She would sooner pen a book than birth a babe, never mind having to engage in despicable intimacies with a male she did not know at all. The thought made her feel nauseous, and she grasped onto the wet wood of the balustrade as a flurry of snow blasted across the structure.

In a moment, he was there, those warm, big hands steadying her—and then he retreated at once to a respectable distance, holding up his hands in silent apology.

She trembled, her heart thundering, her breath clamming up in her chest.

"Is that not what you desire?"

She laughed bitterly. *If only he knew how very much I do not desire it.*

"I thought all ladies dreamed of such things—to marry handsome, rich, powerful lords."

"You insult me, sir, and betray your own false modesty," she said, her words ice cold through clenched teeth.

"Is it a matter for your family?" He furrowed his brow. "Do I need to seek your father's permission to arrange it, or some such thing? I do not know how elven customs work."

"No such thing. I rejected an arrangement of marriage, and my parents united for love. Whenever I see fit, I will arrange my own, though I doubt I ever will. I have no desire to shackle myself to a stranger."

"Well, you have an offer from me, and we are already slightly better than strangers."

"You barely know me," she spat. Did he want her name? That, at least, she could possibly see aligning with the infamous sorcerer, Kassimir the Dark. The Ravakian name was associated with evil, after all. Did he mean to collect it as another to add to the string of his dastardly titles?

"And that, we can change."

"Why?" she bared her teeth at him. "Why me?"

"Why not? Aren't we both of consenting ages? If you do not wish for your family to arrange your marriage, arrange your own. I think you will find me quite *suitable*." There was a gleam of a taunt in his eyes that made her hackles rise.

"I will never put myself at the mercy of male whims. If that is your desire, request something else of me. Anything."

He threw back his head and laughed. "I think you would crawl into my bed before I crawled into yours, little mouse."

She barged past him, but he caught her arm and wheeled her around. She let out a strangled cry of fury, snarling up at his face, so close to hers, and raised a hand to strike him, but he caught her wrist and forced it down. She strained against him, but he was too strong. She could not break free. Angry tears pricked at the corners of her eyes. She felt boiling hot, a fire unable to blaze in his grasp.

"Do not mistake my teasing for ego, Venya." He released her and stepped back stiffly. His voice dropped, all bite gone, all cockiness stripped from him. His gaze burned into her as she stood there, frozen by more than the bitter air.

She would not have heard his next words if she had stood but a few feet away. "You are desperate. You do not stop to consider—so am I."

"I..." *What does he mean?*

"This could work for both of us, Venya. I give you my word. If you agree to marry me on Starfall, I will cure your mother. She will live the rest of her days in good health."

Venya crumpled. He had used her greatest weakness against her. That was what she had come for, after all—a cure for her mother—with the promise of anything as the price. She just did not like what he had asked.

Her body sang with life in that moment, hate and fear,

anger and want. She hated him. And she hated that she was attracted to him. That the closeness between them, the passion of anger, had lit something else within her too. Something that scared her as indefinitely as her responsibility to find a cure for her mother.

She fled.

CHAPTER TWENTY

Kass let her go, even though every ounce of him wanted to hold her back. He leaned heavily on the wooden balustrade, letting the snow pepper cold kisses upon his face, but they were no relief from the feelings rushing through him.

He did not understand this strange elven female. She did not cower before him as she should—as anyone else would. She stood before him, entirely unafraid of him, despite his reputation. He hated how vulnerable that made him feel. How much it made him care for her. She saw him. Gave him a chance. The *real* him, whoever that was, buried under the layers of everything he had been and done, and rumoured to have been and done. She had not despised him until he had divulged his name.

If he did not know any better, he would have sworn she saw right through him. His reputation was nothing but a front, after all, tales spun by others, growing taller in the telling, centuries-old until they bore no more resemblance to him than the swirl of lichen clinging to the frigid wood beside his fingers. He yearned for that understanding, so rare, fragile, and precious. He yearned for *her*.

He sighed and flexed his fingers around the rail, but made no move to follow her. Where could she go? Eventually, they would meet again. She could not leave without his blessing.

Darkness had fallen. His appetite had fled with her, though dinner awaited them both in the dining hall. He wondered if she would make an appearance for it. He did not want to scare her away, if so.

Instead, he stared up at the heavens. The storm had broken at last, the clouds retreating up the peaks to nestle high above the foothills. There was a sliver of night sky and moon tonight to illuminate the now-pale, snow-covered forest valley.

The twin stars, of all the constellations, hung in the cleft. Arielle and Leander.

Of course, they taunt me. He gritted his teeth and dragged a hand through his hair, tearing the bun at his crown loose. Ragged lengths cascaded around his cheeks, the ends catching in his beard.

Their love had been complicated too. Two lovers, one from the heavens and one from earth. A mortal man, fatally injured, saved by the grace of a falling star. Greed had seen her captured, and her mortal lover had endured great trials to see her freed until, in the end, they had ascended to the stars together, safe from the troubles of the world. Wedding on the eve of Starfall had triggered such profound magic it had saved them both.

It was a gloriously hopeful tale and a happy ending, despite the darkness. Was it naïve of him to hope that he could find such peace, too? To hope that he could, in just mere weeks, find an answer? It had been centuries now, and he did not have one.

"Who do you fool? Only yourself…" Ozul said slyly.

Kass could not reply, his throat too thick, for it was true. What a fool he was, to hope a few weeks would make a difference. To hope he could save himself by some miracle—and not just his body but his soul too—from all the darkness it had endured and wrought. To hope he could save her too, instead of sacrificing her.

"You are a fool. Your despair is delicious. Love will not save you, nor an imbecile's hope."

I won't give up, he promised doggedly. *Not until I am entirely out of time and hope. I do not want to kill her. I do not wish her harm.*

"And yet, you will sacrifice her to save your own skin."

The words punctured him and he crumpled, leaning his head on the railing. "I will save so many others by keeping you where you belong; contained."

"Ha! You do not care a damn about them, and you know the truth of it. You are only interested in saving yourself."

The demon's words skewered him. He hated that it was true. That, first and foremost, he cared more about his own skin than anyone else. Yet, was that not what self-preservation entailed? No one else had ever protected Kass—that was up to *him.*

He could not go soft. Not for a pretty face with violet eyes and a heart of gold. Kass did not want to kill her. If he could avoid it, he would. However, saving himself was a must, and he would do anything to ensure his survival.

His thoughts turned to the dark dagger he possessed, now strapped inside his boot. It was a way to cut the demon out, to carve it away from his very soul. He and the demon knew that. It was unconcerned. He did not have the power alone to achieve that. The demon knew that, too.

The blade was also a way to carve out a heart to feed the

demon, soul and all. His chest constricted, breath tight. He did not want to press that to her breast. He was torn, and the damned demon only revelled in his pain.

It was one thing to want to save himself… to consider sacrificing a stranger for his own survival. It was another to have to look into the eyes of someone he knew, someone he already cared for more than he ought to, and exact the price from her.

CHAPTER TWENTY-ONE

*V*enya sat on the window seat in her room, a blanket wrapped around her. The cold stone at her back was a hard tether to the world, for her mind ran elsewhere as she stared up at Arielle and Leander, desperate to escape and reject her tangled feelings.

She could not be attracted to Kassimir the Dark. Could not fall soft to him, despite the shock of those pleading words that had tumbled from his lips.

"'You are desperate. You do not stop to consider—so am I,'" he had said.

Those were not the words of a feared, dastardly sorcerer. But... he was *wrong*. He was kind and generous, gruffly charming and intelligent... and *wrong*. He created malevolent magical constructs. Wrought forbidden grimoires of fire and blood and even practised *necromancy,* if the tales were true. He created the very things she was called to imprison, contain, and sometimes even destroy for public safety.

Furthermore, he bound her with a high price for his help: her hand in order to save her mother. Damned be it, she was so confused.

Venya crumpled and bowed over her raised knees, wrapping her arms around them, her face pressed into the hard bone of her kneecaps beneath the soft blanket.

What should I do?

She had asked the question countless times that evening, but received no answers from herself, the empty room, or the silent stars above.

Thoughts of her mother swam. The last time Venya had seen her, so pale, wasted, and frail in her bed, her bones and nothing more had shown through the ripples in the duvet. So far removed from the strong, vibrant mother that had raised Venya. Terrifyingly so.

It was all her fault. For all that Kassimir had so hotly contested that Venya was blameless, it had been ingrained in her, *by* her, for so many years, she could not escape the weight of that guilt now. The urgency of it all only fuelled her self-loathing.

Hot tears slipped free. This felt so inexorably hopeless, damn it. Venya had worked for *years* to find some kind of solution, to no avail. It was one of the reasons that had driven her to the Athenaeum to become a librarian in the first place. Her love of books and fascination with grimoires had been a significant factor, but *this* was the reason that she would admit to no one.

She had worked so tirelessly, and despite that, she had failed.

Marry me on Starfall. His words chased around her mind.

Had she failed? Perhaps it had all led her here, to this. To him. He had offered her a solution, after all. He had sworn to cure her mother in exchange for her hand. That was an answer and a price. The very answer she wanted, just not for a price she liked. *What is more important? Mother's life, or mine?*

Venya shuddered.

In that, she had her answer. Never mind her own happiness or prospects. Venya had already sacrificed years to answer that question—and she would sacrifice years more if it meant she would, once and for all, be relieved of the terrible burden she had carried. Relieved and punished all in one. Did she deserve happiness, after being the one who had caused her mother such pain?

No, came her answer from the depths of her soul. A union with a stranger far from home. Well, that would be a punishment she ought to bear.

To know Mother was healed… Venya could barely allow herself to dream. She never did. It was usually too hopeless and filled with anguish and guilt. Yet now, hope glimmered in Kassimir's promise. What would it feel like to see her mother whole again? Healthy and strong. Laughing and carefree. Her mother, as she had been in Venya's youth. The vision of those things sprang forth in her mind's eye. Venya's heart ached. What she would give to see that again? She knew the answer.

Anything.

Even herself.

Her mother was worthy of this. She would gladly do it.

Urgency drove her from the window seat, the blanket falling to the stone floor. She had to find Kassimir. Now.

Venya plunged down the stairs, the slippers that Pata had brought her that morning to match this latest dress tapping against each step.

It was dark when she arrived in the hallway below, the wall lamps muted for the night hours. Venya stopped. *Where will he be?* She could find her way to the dining room, but it would be too late for that. She did not recall the way to his drawing room. She had no idea where his private quarters were.

She dithered on the threshold of the tower.

A small flicker of movement to her right jolted her with a rush of fear.

"Are you quite well?"

Venya recoiled and frowned. A fox unfurled from where it had been curled up between the runner carpet and the wall. She did not have time to question this—that there was a fox at the bottom of her stairs or that it could talk. It shimmered with magic too, its coat holding a faint luminescence. She felt that unusual energy exuding from it—the same she had felt from Pata, she realised. *Magical constructs.* Forbidden in Pelenor. Unsurprising, perhaps, in the home of a feared sorcerer. She had already wondered if Pata was a construct or a beast. She ought to be appalled. Instead, hungry curiosity arose.

"I need to find Kassimir."

It stretched and yawned. "Follow me." It set off at a steady lope down the hall, and Venya jogged to keep up.

"What were you doing there?" Venya asked, as much to distract herself as anything else.

"Watching you. Making sure you were safe."

A tingle of cool ran down her back. "Am I in danger?"

"Of course not, but my master wished to be sure of your wellbeing."

"Am I a prisoner?"

The fox spared her glance. "You are a guest."

"What are you?" She followed as it turned down a darker, smaller hall.

"A construct of my master."

As she had guessed. Venya opened her mouth to ask another question, but the fox stopped. Venya halted too, nearly tripping over the hem of her dress. She braced on the wall.

"He will be in there."

With a start, she recognised the door. The drawing room. Softly, she knocked on it.

"It's open," came the reply from within.

Venya paused. She felt dizzy. Her mouth dry, her palms clammy, her pulse skittering, and the hall swimming around her. She had to do this. Venya took a deep, steadying breath, and slipped inside.

Kass lounged inside on one of the armchairs before the fire. Surprise flickered on his face and he straightened at once, abandoning the crystal tumbler on a side table and jumping to his feet. "Venya, I… Are you well?"

Her chest was too tight to reply, and she could not give an honest answer and remain polite. No, she was not well. *Do what must be done, Venya,* she said to herself, straightening her spine and forcing herself to walk to him with measured, even steps.

Before all courage failed her, she had to get it out. "I will marry you on Starfall if you ensure my mother is cured of her heart troubles and obtain proof for me before that date," she blurted. When the words had left her lips, her knees shook, threatening to crumple. She locked her knees. She would not yield.

"I beg your pardon?" he said softly, drawing closer, his eyes wide. The flickering firelight cast shadows across his bearded face, but his eyes held only softness, no anger, no arrogance, no hostility.

"Do not make me repeat it," she said. She could not get the words out again. She would vomit if she had to say more. The room spun and tilted.

Strong hands caught her shoulders, steadying and bracing her. "You're shaking…" He sighed, and slowly lowered her into the chair opposite his, before kneeling at her feet. His hands slipped from her shoulders to clasp hers, now resting in her lap.

The room stopped spinning now that she had firm grounding, and somehow, the contact between them helped slow her frenzied heart and still her erratic breathing.

He sighed. "Venya, I did not mean to pressure you. Only that you and I, we are both desperate souls. This will benefit us both. I will not pressure you into something you do not wish to do." He sounded resigned, sad. His head bowed slightly, as though he worshipped at her feet. His hands did not leave hers.

He looked up. In the firelight, his eyes were molten gold, and his earnest, unfiltered concern made something deep inside her seize.

"What do you wish?" he asked gently.

"I want my mother to be healed." Venya's voice cracked, and the tumultuous emotions within her broke free.

Kassimir's hands moved then. His thumbs wiped away the tears that tumbled with such tenderness that words failed her.

"I will see it done. I swear it to you now thrice on oak, ash, and thorn, that I will heal your mother of her ailment for the fullness of her days and prove it to be so by Starfall."

Venya could not breathe. The weight of her decision crushed her, right though she knew it was, and more tears slipped forth, so many that he could not catch them all. She forced out her promise.

"I swear it to you thrice on oak, ash, and thorn, that I will marry you on Starfall if you do so."

Kassimir stood and, catching her hands once more, pulled her to her feet. She knew what came next. A sealing of their promise. One of his arms wound carefully about her waist, holding her up, for her knees had given out now. She pressed against his firm chest, one hand winding into his shirt—as much to hold herself up as anything else—and her tears freely flowing. That welcoming scent of leather and amber, rich and warm, wafted around her. She hated it in that moment. Hated that it tricked her into comfort.

He cupped her cheek with his other palm, gently pulling her chin up even as he lowered his face to hers. "It shall be done." His hot breath tingled upon her lips, and then his full lips pressed against hers. It was a soft, chaste kiss, but after a moment of warmth, a tingling sear of pleasure-pain sang through her lips. Magic, binding them together in their promise. Venya pulled back with a gasp.

There was something deep in his shadowed gaze that she could not read. Did not want to read. He kept his face bent towards her, the invitation clear. They could continue if she wished it—or not. Something swooped in her belly. A different kind of feeling that wound through the fear and nausea there.

Venya pushed away from him—he released her—and she ran from the room, chased by all her fears. She was now promised to a fae in exchange for the aid of his wicked sorcery.

What have I done?

CHAPTER TWENTY-TWO

Venya's travelling clothes appeared on the chest the next morning, cleaned and folded, alongside another dress, a pretty dove grey thing. Venya ignored the dress and pulled on her leggings appreciatively—she would always choose practicality and comfort first—before braiding her hair in a plait that fell to her waist. Once dressed, she descended to the hallway—now empty of the fox construct—and made her way to breakfast.

She had barely slept, tossing and turning all night, her thoughts tumbling like stones upon a riverbed, knocking together but never settling until dawn had cracked and she had entirely forsaken the attempt. Now, her head was thick, her limbs heavy, and her eyes swollen and gritty. A river of anxiety ran through her belly, but she had not eaten in so many hours she felt ravenous despite her nerves.

She was promised to a fae in marriage.

The thought had grown no less daunting overnight.

He awaited her in the dining room, his chin resting upon clasped hands, his gaze unseeing as he stared into nowhere. Her footsteps faltered.

At the scuff on the floor, Kassimir started and looked up at her. He stood. "Good morning, Venya." It was softer than she expected, though still with a bite of what seemed to be his customary gruffness.

"Good morning." That nausea roiled in her belly anew as she forced herself to step to the table. As he had done before, Kassimir pulled out her chair, waited for her to sit, and tucked her in. Her eyes scrunched shut as she forced down the hot sting of tears. He was unfailingly polite. Why did that only seem to make this more difficult?

He poured her a cup of sweet tea and waited until she had helped herself to a piece of toast before he too partook of the stack.

"I thought after we have broken fast, I should not delay in fulfilling my part of our… arrangement," he murmured. "I spent the night preparing a cure for your mother."

She whipped her attention to him, the half-eaten toast forgotten in her hand. She swallowed the dry mouthful. "Already?" Her heart panged. He had not slept either—she could not tell it from his visage, but for a slight shadow under his eyes, perhaps—but for her?

"From what you showed me, and from your own fervour, there is no time to be lost."

"Thank you. It is weeks of travel, though." Venya dropped the toast and cradled her face in her hands, her hope curdling. "It may not reach her by Starfall. It shall be too late." That was the truth she did not dare admit to herself. She had already spent too long on the road and would not be able to reach home in time.

"It will not. I have means to send it far quicker."

Her hands fell and her hope leapt. "Truly?"

"I can have it to your mother within the week." His expression was grave, but a spark of mischief tinged by bitterness crossed his eyes and graced his lips with a quick smile. "Dark fae sorcerer, remember?"

Her answering smile faded just as quickly. *Do not forget who you dwell with now. Do not forget who owns you. Remember why.*

Venya could eat no more. Starving though she was, she felt too sick to master another bite. Her tea had gone cold.

Kassimir stood, after silently determining that she was done, and invited her to follow him. He led her down unfamiliar halls and steps, lower, into the bowels of the place, until the scent of damp rose and the hallway windows suggested they were at ground level. He led her through a locked wooden door punctured by iron studs that required three keys and two doses of magic to open. They passed into a large circular room that rose three stories to a vaulted wooden roof above, softly illuminated by rising arrow slits.

As she stepped across the threshold, the temperature plunged. Those arrow slits were open to the winter. She shivered and rubbed her hands together, blowing on them.

Venya's attention rose to that and then fell to the assortment of workbenches and shelves around the perimeter of the room. They held all manner of strange things in glass bottles and jars, scrolls, and one cabinet of tiny drawers that she longed to explore but did not dare to. From where she stood, she could not read the handwritten labels on each drawer. Curiosity had her turning on the spot, her host forgotten.

"This is my workshop," Kassimir said. He crossed to a bench and picked up a small vial. "Here. This is what your mother needs."

Venya followed and took it gingerly from his hands. The fragile crystal was cold upon her fingertips. It felt so insubstantial. She carefully examined the fire-coloured liquid inside. It slipped from one end of the vial to the other quite smoothly as she tilted it, glittering with magic in the faint light.

"This will heal her?" It seemed so insubstantial.

"It will. I have instructions for its administration. One teaspoon on the first day, followed by a single drop each day until the vial is finished. It shall suffice." He gestured to a small scroll tightly rolled up and sealed with a wax wrap. "She should improve noticeably within days, and in a month, be healed well enough to resume her activity. No doubt she will be quite wasted away after such a convalescence."

Venya nodded and swallowed. "Thank you. Are there any ill side effects?"

"None. She will not bear any ill consequences from taking this." His tone was level, serious.

Her glance flicked to him. He appeared sincere.

"I suggest that you pen a letter to send alongside it, an explanation. I doubt a gift from an unknown source will make it to your mother."

"Of course." That made sense. And it would give her a chance to say what she could not say in person too. Her stomach lurched. Would she ever see her mother again? They had discussed no terms of this arranged marriage. Would she be expected to remain here? A prisoner, perhaps? Would she be permitted to travel? A prickle climbed up the nape of her neck.

"Venya?"

She blinked. He held out a quill to her, his brow crinkled.

She cleared her throat and stepped forward to take it. Her jaw fell. "Is this a...?"

"Phoenix feather. Yes." He gave her a lopsided grin and turned back to the table to drag a sheet of parchment closer for her. "It was a rare find."

Venya stroked along its length, feeling the softness of the feather and the strange fizzling tingle as it traversed her skin. Oranges and scarlets, golds and even magentas graced it, bright and glossy. She dipped the tip into the ink well that Kassimir had placed next to the parchment and paused.

What could she say? What in Pelenor could she pen that would give voice to the depth of her emotion? She chewed her lip as she struggled for words. This letter meant *everything.*

Shadows shifted beside her, and she felt Kassimir draw away. A moment later she heard the clatter of wood on glass, the rattle of jars, as he busied himself. She wondered if he was just being kind to give her space.

Venya did not know how long it took her to pen that letter, but eventually, she straightened, groaning as her stiff back protested at how she had hunched over the table to write. She cleaned off the quill on a rag and placed it neatly on the desk, wiping her ink-spattered fingers too. She scanned the letter. Those words felt too few to convey the depth of what she felt. It was impossible to add more. She had filled the parchment front and back.

"I'm done," she said quietly.

Kassimir returned to her side at once. "As you wish." He took the parchment—and she appreciated that he did not attempt to read it—and folded it up into ever-decreasing squares, until he had a bundle no larger than his palm. He wrapped it with twine and sealed it with wax and magic. "Now for the messenger. Alas. I did not have time to make him, the medicine for your mother took all night."

He said it casually with no dig at her, nothing to inspire guilt, but it elicited it, nonetheless. She was not used to people doing her such kindnesses. It drew something else forth too, a tenderness that made her chest ache.

"Thank you," she whispered.

"Come." He drew her to one side of the workshop and gestured to a stool pulled to one side of the table there. "Sit, please."

She shivered as a gust of wind blew through one of the arrow slits high above and filtered down in a swirl. Kassimir tutted and reached for a length of dark fabric hung on the wall by an iron peg nailed between the stones. A cloak.

"Here." He held it, waiting for her to step forward, and wrapped it around her shoulders.

The warm, thick fabric cut off the chill immediately, and enveloped her in the scent of cloves and wood smoke. She sank appreciatively onto the stool and watched as he arranged an array of oddities on the table and the ground around him, from sprigs of herbs to crystals to powders and all manner of things she did not recognise.

At last, he had a circle of things around him and an array marked out in ash and chalk on the flagstones at his feet. Lines intersecting, curves swirling, characters floating— sorcery she had only ever read about, but never witnessed.

Her own skin tingled as she felt his rising power flower through the room. He stood there, head tipped back, face to the sky, his hair swept back in that neat knot and his arms outstretched to the sides as though he offered himself up. And then, he began to *glow*. It illuminated his skin softly at first, then more intently, and she had to squint as the symbols upon the floor burst into light and fire too and rose from the floor to swirl around him until he seemed lost in a cocoon of power.

He was *glorious*, glowing with power and radiant as he basked in it, channelling it through him with ease. She could not tear her attention from him. The forbidden sorcery ought to have felt abhorrent, but instead, it called to her soul with a wild abandon she longed to answer. Venya's hands gripped the side of the stool. Warmth and excitement charged through her, her natural curiosity entirely enthralled by the spectacle before her.

Venya watched as he plucked golden and amber lines from the air amidst swirling motes of light, forming them into a shape that was too bright to make out. So absorbed by him, she could not say how long he worked, as the form took shape painstakingly slowly.

At last, she felt something *snap* as though a threshold had been met, and a ripple ran through the magic there, passing through her with a warm shiver. She gasped as the magic surrounding Kassimir fell away.

CHAPTER TWENTY-THREE

enya watched as the tumbling magic revealed Kassimir in all his wild glory. He grinned with utter abandon, those fangs gleaming and his silver eyes entirely amber in the light of his sorcery. An invisible breeze, one of magic, whipped the fabric of his shirt, billowing, tugging and teasing loose strands of his hair. Last of all, he closed those eyes for a long moment and breathed magic deeply onto what he had made.

On one outstretched arm now stood an eagle, entirely constructed of magic, and as that fan of magic-laced breath hit it, it solidified from a web of glowing golden threads into a corporeal form. Its gaze locked with Kassimir's until the last of the magic fell away, and then it squawked, shaking its head and flaring out its wings. It was so huge in wingspan that Venya startled and leaned back on her chair, certain one of those wing tips would catch her.

"Easy," crooned Kassimir, and turned to Venya, giving her a triumphant grin. His eyes held a wildness that excited and scared her, and a ripple fluttered low in her stomach. "Meet your messenger, milady."

"Extraordinary," whispered Venya. She leaned closer. The bird appeared entirely solid and corporeal, just like the panther and fox constructs, the telltale lace of magic sparkling along its feathers the only hint of sorcery visible to the naked eye. When she felt it with her magic, it seemed entirely different. No life within it could she sense, hollow it was in that regard, but it was formed and filled with magical energy.

"It will not peck you." He sounded almost amused and twisted to hold the bird closer to her as it folded its wings tightly against its body.

She reached out a hesitant hand and gasped when her fingers connected with soft, warm feathers. "It feels so real."

The bird swivelled its head to regard her with one golden orb. It made no move to attack, retreat, or lean into her touch.

He smiled. "It is, just not in the living fashion." He crossed to where her parchment rested on the desk and set the bird down next to it. It hopped from his arm, its claws scratching on the worn wood.

So real. She wondered at it for a moment longer before watching him tie that precious parcel—the letter and vial—into a bundle and then onto the eagle's leg.

At his beckoning gesture, she followed him outside with the bird on his arm, along that damp-filled corridor and out of a side door into a courtyard she had not yet seen. Snow from the overnight storm banked waist high on one side of the yard, where the wind had created a drift. Kassimir ventured to the shallower end, where their feet crunched only an inch deep into the unbroken white covering. Venya was glad for her boots now. Slippers would have been entirely unsuitable.

"Where am I to send him?" Kassimir turned to her. The

bird looked to the sky but made no move to leave. "If I may have perhaps a mental recollection of your journey to your required destination, that would be most helpful. The bird can travel it in reverse."

"Of course."

He held out his hand and she took it, stiffening at the warmth that flooded through her cold hand from him—and at the tendril of questioning thought that he sent to her. She latched onto that tendril and scrunched her eyes shut, sending her consciousness to him, reliving the journey in reverse from point to point.

A tug of grief yanked at her chest as she sent him memories from her direct point of view. Her journey had been spent entirely upon Boy's broad back. And now he was gone. In the tumultuousness of the past days—the number of which she had entirely lost track of, but it had to have been a week or more, since the barrow wight attack upon the road —she had not had the space to think of him, let alone mourn his passing or flagellate herself with blame for it. Perhaps that was a blessing, for now, that grief and guilt drowned her anew.

Kassimir's hand gripping firmly onto hers was the only thing that kept her anchored in that present moment as he took her memories all the way north, back to Pelenor and further still, up to the top reaches of the country to the summer palace, her family's main residence away from court in the capital. A beautiful haven of peace where her mother now spent all her time with the healers.

There, their connection ended. He pulled away gently and released her hand. Venya opened her eyes. The ghost of his touch and heat lingered, painfully sensitive. She pulled her hand beneath the folds of her borrowed, too-long cloak, her breath shuddering through her chest.

Kassimir closed his eyes and bent his forehead to rest upon the eagle's head. It watched him, unblinking. She felt a small trickle of magic flow from him to the construct—and then he straightened and held his arm up. With a large, sweeping movement, the eagle unfurled its wings and launched.

It called, the shriek biting through her, and rose with powerful wingbeats, circling until it was little more than a speck amongst the clouds. Then, it turned north and sped into the distance.

Her neck ached from craning to watch it. It was just a dot in the sky above the mountains and forests, filling with a tangle of emotions as it drew further away. And then, it was gone.

She watched, and kept watching, but she saw nothing more. Still, she stared up into the sky. That bird carried all her hope and took a piece of her heart with it. Her shoulders slumped as she finally relented. It would do her little good to stand there waiting for that slow chill to creep through her. She could not feel her toes, good boots be damned.

Kassimir stood behind her to one side, a silent, warm, and solid presence at her back. Waiting. She wondered, for her? He made no move to rush her.

She turned to him. "It will definitely reach her?" Her heart hurt with the weight of feelings—fear, grief, worry, guilt.

"It will. I enchanted it to fly faster than the prevailing winds. Nothing shall stop it until it reaches its destination— and returns to us with a message confirming the safe delivery of its package. Then, and only then, will the magic holding it together unlock and dissipate."

Her shoulders sagged with relief at the surety in his tone and his posture. He had no doubts whatsoever. In that, she could trust a little more than her own unfounded and rising worries. A weight felt as though it had been lifted from her shoulders as she had watched that bird and its precious cargo vanish over the horizon.

She had a cure for her mother. It had not unfolded in the manner she had expected—her meeting with Kassimir, her discovery of his identity, and the bargain now between them to secure what she needed… but she had it. And the relief scoured out the heavy weight that had sat upon her chest. The next breath she drew felt deeper and fresher.

CHAPTER TWENTY-FOUR

Kass watched the weight drop from her shoulders as they sent that construct into the skies. It touched a deep part of him—the part he had pretended did not exist for so long now. The shred that cared for others, painful though that was. Something in him had lifted too when she thanked him and he felt the potent tang of her emotion.

It made him want to be better. This caring, it felt dangerous. He wanted her to see that he wasn't so bad.

"Even though you are. You will be the death of her..." came the inner voice he could not escape.

I will find a way to cleave you from my soul and end you, Ozul, Kass vowed.

"She will discover soon enough the truth of your dark and accursed soul, Kassimir."

No, she won't. His answer was stubbornness and nothing of substance. They both knew it. He had been trying to save himself for long enough, to no avail. The odds he could save her too were even slimmer.

Kass led Venya inside back to the warmer parts of the

castle where, after a hungry morning's work, they both fell into silence as they devoured sandwiches of crusty thick bread, still ever so slightly warm, slathered with fresh butter and filled with slices of salty, honey-roasted ham and fresh cheese. When hot milk with cocoa powder appeared on the table, hot and steaming, something low in his stomach pulled as she let out a small moan filled with appreciative delight.

Stop it, he admonished himself. She had made her intentions entirely clear. They had discussed no terms of their arrangement, but she had stated that she desired no husband or partner. That the very thought repulsed her. Much as he could not deny that he was attracted to her, he would not do anything she did not wish. He was that decent, at least. It was a small mark in the redeeming features column of his personality. The thought amused him, though it quickly soured.

She slouched in the chair, that hot steaming mug clutched between both hands and held close to her chest. "This is divine. We only have this at the Yule festival at home. It's so rare and difficult to get a hold of. Thank you." She smiled at him, the first relaxed smile he had truly received from her. Maybe she was not so hostile to him as he dreaded. His fragile confidence lifted a little.

All the same, his tongue felt too thick and clumsy to reply. Kass swallowed, cleared his throat, and made a noncommittal sound of acknowledgement. His cheeks felt hot as he turned back to his plate, picking up a morsel of cheese that had fallen from his sandwich and devouring it. It melted upon his tongue.

"Would you like me to escort you on a tour?" he offered, wiping his clammy palms upon his knees under the table, hoping she would not notice the movement. "You came here in the night and have barely seen anything of the place. If you are to remain here—" He winced as she blanched. "Ahem. I mean, if this is to become your home," he rephrased carefully. She did not look any more at ease, "Then it is only fitting you should know every hall. Besides, I promised you the library." He gave her what he hoped was a reassuring smile.

Her answering one was wan, driven more by politeness he reckoned than willingness.

"Of course."

The library, he decided. She would like that best, if books were her vocation. He led her there, pausing outside the vast panelled wooden door. He spent more time in his workshop making his constructs and grimoires than he did in there with the collection. Perhaps with her here, that would change. He crushed that daydream before it could bloom.

She stepped over the threshold. He followed and had to stop or risk crashing into her, for she had halted, gasping with wonder. He watched as she gaped, taking it all in. He supposed it would be impressive for a newcomer—perhaps he took it for granted. He tried to look at it through her eyes. What would she admire? Perhaps the ribbed, vaulted ceiling, in the same style as her bedroom ceiling, only this was painted a deep scarlet between the pale stone ribs, and decorated with swirling vines of gold. Metal casings ornamented with wrought flourishes housed faelights that never went out, casting the room in a soft, warm glow.

Dark mahogany shelves stretched the length of the long room, windows above them taking the ceiling height up and adding extra room to what would otherwise have been an oppressive space. Some of those shelves were caged and locked, with their angry inhabitants kicking up a raucous stink at their entrance. Kass was not in the practice of restraining grimoires, but he had created some nasty ones over the years. He had no intention of giving them free run of his home.

He slammed the door neatly behind them as Venya shrieked and leapt out of the way of the grimoire that came scurrying on little clawed feet, barrelling straight towards the exit. He scooped it up, holding it at arm's length as it quivered and yowled and gobbled at him.

"Nice try. Not this time. Go on." He tossed it onto the top of the nearest shelf where it screamed obscenities at him and then retreated into a shadowed corner, growling.

"My apologies." He turned to Venya, who had leapt onto a chair to escape. She stared at it, wild-eyed. And then around at the rest of the room where grimoires freely moved around non-sentient books shelved and stationary.

"You let them out on purpose?" she said, her voice hushed. She did not seem scared, more curious, he would have said.

"They won't hurt you. Not with me here." He offered a hand and helped her down.

"Sorry," she muttered, her cheeks blooming red. He bit back a smile.

"That's quite alright. I did not warn you."

She looked at him, a brow quirked, waiting for an answer.

"These are my creations. Why would I not give them freedom?"

"You don't give those freedom." She nodded towards the secured shelves.

"Yes, well, there are exceptions to every rule." He glared at that shelf darkly. "Those are safer behind bars, believe me." *If I let some of those out, this castle would be reduced to rubble, and we'd be dead.*

He had made it a source of pride in his foolish youth to create such dangerous and powerful tomes. "The door stays shut for that reason. The rest have the freedom of this place. They cannot leave."

Venya drifted into the room, stopping to examine a sleeping grimoire that snored on the corner of a desk, a fur and claw-covered tome that was one of his tamer creations. She edged carefully away before she spoke.

"Fascinating. Did you create all these?" He could not discern if her gaze was critical or curious.

"Aye."

"That's impressive. More than impressive. I've never seen such a number in a private collection before." She turned and wandered down the gallery—he kept pace behind her, not wanting her to fall afoul of his collection. He could not remember all that he had created, truth be told. Or how malevolent they were.

One darted out, spitting globs of something viscous that burned holes in the rug under their feet.

He growled and surged forward, but Venya was already there with a wave of her own magic that sent slumber crashing over the little beastie. It fell, cover thudding open, onto the carpet and was still, the only movement a slight fluttering of its pages.

Kass blinked at her as a tinge of smoke from the ruined carpet threatened to make him sneeze.

Venya turned to him, a slight air of mischief about her smirk—one that made his stomach flip. "I can handle a few badly behaved grimoires. Trust me."

Kass chuckled. "Alright. Well, there is the non-chaotic library, too." They left, Kass ensuring not a creation slipped out before he closed the door.

He spent the day showing her around the place from the non-magical library, where she lingered for an hour, examining the two storeys of shelving in the peaceful space, to the gardens, subdued and pruned for winter, to each of the three courtyards, now covered in drifting snow, and the open tower. On a clear day, mountains crowned the north, east, and south, and the west stretched into the Wildwood and eventually other realms. They remained up there for mere minutes before the cold chased them down again, for they both had forgotten cloaks and a fresh storm approached.

He took her to the kitchen next, where dishes cleaned themselves and pots bubbled on the stove. The scent of fresh bread laced the air, making his mouth water.

"You sustain all this yourself?" Somehow her frown contained wonder.

"Yes." His spirit soured. "Terrible and maligned sorcerer, remember? I do not get many visitors. Fewer still wish to remain here."

Her head drooped a little—he wondered if she regretted that *she* would have to remain here—and she nodded.

"Do not worry, delicious elf. You will not remain here for long," crooned the demon, hammering another nail into his heart. Kass smashed it back down into that box with unbridled savagery.

"Are you alright?" she asked.

He turned to her and forced the thunderous scowl from his face. "Fine. Cold. Shall we have a hot cocoa?"

Her face lit at that. "Please. I cannot feel my fingers after our outdoor adventures."

He prepared two cups of hot milk, warming it through with magic, before stirring in the cocoa powder and handing her a mug.

She took it with a grateful sigh. "That's better."

"Tell me, what part of the castle did you like best today? There is more yet to show you."

"The library." Her face cracked into a grin. "*Both* of them, for different reasons. There is so much peace—and chaos too in the other, I suppose. I should like to study everything inside them in great detail."

Something in his heart hurt to see her so brightly happy. It could not last. Both he and the damned demon inside him knew that. The day's affairs had been a mere distraction, but the bitter, dastardly truth remained and she was blind to it.

"Then, they are yours," he blurted, to cease that internal flow of self-destruction. "The libraries. Now and forever. Do with them as you wish."

She blinked at him, and then her surprise softened into a smile of such shy sweetness he hated himself even more for it.

He relieved her of the now empty mug, took her hand, and bent to brush a kiss upon her knuckles. "Consider it a gift of my goodwill, Venya. I wish for nothing more than your happiness here." It was the truth. His heart raged inside him, anguish-filled and aching. There had to be a way to save himself that did not end in her demise. He could not bear it.

She did not pull her hand away or recoil from him, and so he released it with reluctance, guilt roiling through him.

He would find a way to free himself of this demon, without sacrificing this young woman he was growing to enjoy far too much. He had to find a way.

"It is impossible, my dearest Kassimir. You and I both know it. In days, she will be dead and I will feast on you both before I take on the world..."

CHAPTER TWENTY-FIVE

enya's heart was full to bursting with *hope*, and it was so foreign she did not know whether to drown in its heady intoxication or retreat in fear at such unfamiliarity. A cure winged its way to her mother at that very second, mere days away, if that, and despite her fears over her arrangement with Kassimir, he continued to behave so differently than she had expected.

Far from the dark and vicious sorcerer she had expected, he treated her with such open respect it *hurt*. He seemed to genuinely seek to please her.

They are yours, he had said of those libraries. *Now and forever.*

Something within him had tightened at those words—said with such generous fervour—and when he had taken her hand and kissed it so gently. Was he so terrible? She doubted it more and more. Had she still not known his identity, had he used a false moniker, she would have been none the wiser. Were the tales all false? For before her stood an irresistibly handsome fae male with an equally inviting personality, equal parts gruff and mysterious, warm and kind.

When he dropped her hand, disappointment curdled. Self-loathing rose at the recognition of that feeling. This was a business arrangement, no more. A punishment for what she had done to her mother.

You're not supposed to enjoy this. You're not supposed to be attracted to him.

She was supposed to endure this stoically. So why did it feel all too easy to just be herself around him, free of judgement? So easy to enjoy his company and the wonders of his home—now hers too, she supposed.

His attention burned her. They stood close in the kitchen, the cups forgotten on the side. The look in his amber-silver eyes held her. *Does he feel something too?* The intensity of it dizzied her.

Before either of them could break the moment, a shriek rang out. There, in the heart of the place, they ought not have heard anything through the thick stone, but this cry had travelled on that magical plane that permeated everything.

At once, Kass stiffened and his eyes flicked north, his body angling towards the source of that call.

"What was that?" Venya asked.

"A breach," Kass growled. In an instant, he grew darker and more threatening. The very shadows in that dimly lit space seemed to yawn and stretch, and a tingle of fear stroked down Venya's spine. "I must go."

"I want to come." Venya's heart hammered. She did not know what she wanted, but she did not want to leave his side. That cry had set her on edge. If there was danger, she did not want to wait alone in this unfamiliar place.

Kass's mouth worked soundlessly. A groan escaped—a sign of his own choice. "Fine. I do not have time to argue. I may yet need your sorcery. My own is still depleted." Without warning, he stepped closer until they stood chest to chest. His arms gathered around her, a tight but comforting cage, and then the world fell away as he stepped into shadow and wind.

A moment later and they stepped into the world again. Venya's head reeled. She had heard of shadow walking—her father was an expert, her mother competent—but it was not something she had ever attempted or experienced. Or wanted to. She was grateful for his unyielding grasp to steady her. After a moment, her blackened vision faded with the dizziness, and she pushed out of his arms.

He strode away at once with a cry. "Imperion!"

Venya's breath caught. A horse—no, a centaur—lay upon the ground. *It's not Boy*, she had to tell herself, swallowing down a rising tide of nausea and forcing herself to advance. She sent out her senses and paused. There was no life here. No death—but no life. Just magic.

A construct!

She rushed to Kass's side and dropped to her knees beside him. The centaur was huge, even prone on the ground. Long dark hair and a beard tumbled in braids down a bare chest, also swirling with dark hair that flowed into the body of a shadow-coloured stallion.

"A darkness came down from the mountains," the creature said in a deep, rasping voice. "I tracked it for two days—to here—but it was stronger than I. It bested me. I have failed you, Kass." The mighty centurion shifted on the ground. A ripple of hair moved, and Venya gasped as it revealed a gaping wound upon the centurion's neck, slashing south across its chest and stomach. No blood, however, she could instead see a tear in the very structure of the construct, the edges raw like ripped fabric and sparking with magic that leaked into the ether instead.

"You did not fail me, friend," Kass said, sighing. "I bear

responsibility for these abominations." He turned to Venya. "Help me, will you?"

She nodded, and he took her hand, placing his other across that fissure upon Imperion's chest. She sucked in a breath as she felt him pull the magic from her. She watched with fascination as Imperion's magical flesh knitted together. She had some, albeit old, experience of healing such deep wounds—working with grimoires required some training and experience, for there was always the risk of injuries—but constructs, forbidden as they were, were entirely out of her experience.

Imperion groaned with relief as the breach joined. "Thank you, Kass."

Kass left his hand upon Imperion's chest a moment longer. Venya felt the tug on her magic cease to just the smallest trickle. Kass made sure Imperion was entirely healed. Then, he squeezed her hand in silent thanks, and stood, helping her up.

Around them, the forest was silent, clad in a carpet of white that stretched between the evergreen trees. No hint of anything untoward, except where they were. There, the snow was churned into muck, marring the illusion of peace.

At their feet, Imperion rolled onto his belly and staggered to his feet. Across his hips, slung above his forelegs, a bandolier of weaponry hung. He checked over his weapons—throwing daggers, a sword, a broadsword, and arrows. One arrow had cracked, and he examined it with a grumble of frustration. Where he had fallen on the ground, however...

Imperion swore.

There lay a crushed wooden bow, fractured beyond use, the two split pieces of the wooden limb attached by a string. "I can make another, but it will take weeks."

"There will be a spare of some kind in the castle. I will see that you have it," Kass said, but his attention was not on Imperion. He twisted on the spot, scanning the trees around them.

"It is long gone, Kass."

"I will find it." His voice held a grim promise that made Venya shiver. That shiver did not cease. It was cold, and they had left without cloaks. The winter chill crept into her, and not even a blast of her magic to warm herself could stave it off for long.

Kass turned to her. "Venya, you must return to the castle with Imperion. It is not safe for you out here. If a demon has come down from the mountain, my lands are not safe until it is ended."

"Are *you* safe?" she asked. It came out before she had time to think about it. Her cheeks warmed.

Kass's eyes softened. "I am well used to this life, Venya. Please. Go with Imperion. He will keep you safe, and I shall not worry for you if I know where you are. I will return, but first, I must hunt."

Worry kept her breaths shallow. Worry for her, for Imperion… and for *him*. "Please take care."

His throat bobbed and his reply was thick. "I will." He raised a hand and brushed her cheek with a knuckle. "Now go, *please*."

Imperion sank onto his forelocks and offered her an arm to mount him. She gritted her teeth as Imperion surged to his feet and wrapped her arms around his waist. She had never ridden bareback, or on a centaur before, but there was no time to adjust, for Imperion spun and surged away from Kass, plunging into the depths of the forest with Venya on his back. She turned. But Kass was already gone.

CHAPTER TWENTY-SIX

Kass returned long after the onset of night, aching and tired to his bones. He had chased chase one demon—and eliminated it—but there had been two trails. The other had led him on a wild chase to nowhere, and eventually, he had to concede defeat and circle back.

Concern punched through his fatigue. They were inside the wards of his realm. It grew worse month on month—and lately, week on week—making the waning of his strength too tangible for him to deny. It was not safe for Venya here, not truly, and despite that, he was the greatest danger to her of all. He could not bear it.

Are the wards on the castle safe? He questioned that, too. The Darkyn drew nearer with every incursion onto his lands. The wards upon his home were strongest of all and yet doubt clouded his mind.

A light awaited as he strode into the main courtyard, casting a warm glow through the glass onto the snow. Pata lurked inside the main door, sleeping on the hearthrug in the hallway as he always did when his master remained out. The big cat stretched as Kass entered and yawned, showing gigantic teeth.

"It's about time."

"I could have used your help out there," Kass grumbled.

"Yes, well, I was here, as you well know, tending to equally important matters." Pata nudged his head towards the armchair there. Normally, it was a glorified stool for Kass to take his boots off. Tonight, it was full.

Venya slumbered there, her body curled up on the chair, feet tucked under her, and her cheek leaned into the wing.

Kass forgot his retort in an instant and crossed to the chair. "Is she well?" he whispered.

"She could not sleep. I found her wandering the halls like a lost lamb. She insisted she could not rest until you returned safely, so we waited here. As you can see, your tardiness found both of us breaking that promise."

"She cannot stay here. What a blasted uncomfortable place to sleep." Kass chewed his lip.

"I always knew you were a great big softy."

Kass glared at the big cat, who lashed his tail in silent, defiant answer. He had been thinking, before walking in the door, of sleeping on the floor beneath Venya's tower, just for that night, just to be sure she was safe. It was as close as he dared—he would have preferred her chamber floor, seeing as that would ensure her complete security, but he did not want her waking up to such an unexpected surprise. One that she would, no doubt, despise.

He swayed with tiredness. "Blast it," he grumbled to himself.

She murmured and stirred in the chair. There was nothing for it. He bent towards her, cupping a shoulder gently with one hand. "Venya?" he said softly.

She woke, unfocused eyes opening to regard him, before

she came to properly and sat up, gasping. "I fell asleep! Pata! You ought to have woken me." She shot a look of such reproach at the big cat, it made Kass want to laugh. He managed a tired smile.

"It's not my fault," defended Pata. "I fell asleep too." He sniffed. "And I do not appreciate the interruption to *my* sweet dreams. Good night." With that, he stalked down the hall, tail flicking.

"You need not have waited up for me," Kass said.

Venya stood, groaning and grimacing as she unfolded from her cramped position on the chair. "I could not sleep. I was… too worried." Those last two words were barely louder than a whisper.

Kass's throat closed. He could not reply.

"Did you achieve what you set out to?" She glanced up at him. Dark shadows hollowed her eyes. He wondered if his own mirrored them. He felt utterly drained and longed for his bed, but he would not see it that night. Not if she agreed to his proposal.

"In part. Come. We must go to bed. There were two… intruders." He did not want to bring mention of demons into his home that night. "I hunted one. The other escaped. I am being overly cautious, but I wish to check the wards upon this place come the dawn. Ensure they are all secure. Ironclad.

"Until then, I will not leave you unattended. Since Pata has seen fit to abandon your side, I shall remain with you. I have not renewed the wards on your tower for years—you will take my chamber tonight. It is the only space kept regularly reinforced."

He could not tell her why—a precaution against the demon inside him. *Let her think it for my own protection.* "It is the only space I trust you to remain safe."

Something flickered across her face too fast for him to read.

"I will be there too," he added carefully, "but I will not share the bed."

Not unless you wish me to, he wanted to add, but dared not. A tumble between the sheets would have been an enjoyable pastime on any other night. That night, he longed for nothing more than to fall into a deep and nightmare-free slumber—with her curled against his chest, if he were being entirely honest with himself. He did not say it. He did not offer it. He did not want to witness her rejection, and he was certain he would receive it if he were foolish enough to ask her.

Kass waited. He stood a few feet away from her. The space felt intimate, but a gulf hung between them.

Eventually, she nodded, her gaze lingering on the pooling shadows around them. "Alright. If you think that wise."

He breathed around the growing tightness in his chest. "I do. Come."

CHAPTER TWENTY-SEVEN

*V*enya's heart thundered as she followed Kass to his bed chamber. This was all so unexpected, and she had no inkling how to process any of it, save to keep meeting the surprises head-on that seemed to spring forth every day in this place and from him.

Kassimir's chambers were pitch black.

He illuminated the lamps with a swirl of magic, providing a dim light. It was entirely different to her cosy, high-ceilinged tower room. This room was all Kass. Dark drapes hung on the walls. Long curtains of black velvet obscured the windows. A glittering chandelier overhead remained unlit. Against the far wall, an ornate four-poster bed stood, draped in obsidian black fabrics chased with silver embroidery. At the foot, an ottoman with clothes strewn on it and a pair of boots beside it, one fallen over.

This was his inner sanctum. Venya stepped inside, her mouth dry, her tongue thick, her chest tight. Nerves washed over her. They still had not discussed the terms of their arrangement. Any physical limitations. She had barely considered it—save to brush her worries aside. Would this chamber one day be hers? *Theirs?*

She had sensed no ulterior motives from him with his invitation to retreat there. It was the only driving reason she had agreed. He had not forced himself upon her in any way thus far, and his actions had been consistently respectful. She realised, as she crossed the threshold and the door snapped shut behind them with a flicker of magic, which let slip the wards guarding the place, that she was not scared of him. That she trusted him, like she had trusted no male before. That, in itself, unnerved her.

"I must wash this filth off me," said Kassimir. He strode to another door and opened it to reveal a grand bathroom. Venya peered in nosily. A giant beaten copper bathtub filled the room.

Kassimir stripped off his shirt, revealing a bronzed back knotted with rippling muscles and chased with silvery scars. Venya's breath caught, and she whirled away, heart hammering, before he caught her staring. He had no modesty—but that did not extend to her. She still wore her clothes, and now she realised her error. She had nothing to wear for bed. Undressing was out of the question.

She steeled herself. "Kassimir?"

"Yes?" He turned, giving her a view of… She looked up at his face immediately, her cheeks on fire. Heavens damn it, she couldn't breathe or think straight. Why did he have to be so attractive? That did *not* help matters, especially if they were supposed to spend the night in the same room. She harboured absolutely no assumptions—days ago, for goodness' sake, she had never thought she would marry, and here she was in an arrangement of convenience—but that did not mean she was oblivious or unwanting.

"I-I don't have anything to wear for bed." In her tower room, there had been a light nightdress to wear.

Kassimir smiled tiredly. "If I were in the mood, I'd suggest nothing," he said, letting out a dry chuckle and throwing her a darkly suggestive look. "But I think you would throw something at me, so I had better not. Look in the ottoman. There'll be one of my clean shirts in there. On you, it will be a nightgown."

Venya rummaged through the chest, her heart pounding at his casual flirtation. The sounds of running water and splashing came from the bathroom. She dug out a white linen shirt that seemed suitable and stood. Kass entered, a towel wrapped around his waist. A line of dark hair sank from his navel out of sight under the fabric.

"You can go in there to wash and change." He jabbed a thumb at the bathroom. "I suppose I shall put on some trousers for you."

Venya's cheeks warmed yet again. She scurried into the bathroom to wash her face, relieve herself, and change. With her clothes bundled, she slipped out. Kass was, to her relief, wearing some light trousers as he had promised, and had taken some of the many pillows from the bed onto the fur rug before the fire, which he had lit.

It looked cosy. "I don't mind taking the floor," she offered. "I've slept in far worse places."

"Nonsense. You take the bed. I am not so despicable that I have lost all sense of chivalry." He glanced at her, a brow raised, but he froze at the sight of her, his lips parted as he took her in.

Venya inclined her head and crossed to the bed hurriedly, all too aware of her bare legs exposed beneath the hem of his shirt, and the way it left so little to the imagination. She slipped between the covers, biting back a groan. The bed smelled of *him*. Musk and amber, warm and rich, vanilla and spice, she would reek of him tomorrow too. Venya gritted her teeth. *No matter.*

Kass arranged himself on that fur pelt, no blanket to cover him, his body angled to the fire, his back to her.

"Good night." Exhaustion washed over her as her body sank into the soft, comfortable bed. She needed rest. Still not yet recovered from the wight attack—that wightmark a pale brand on her throat—and depleted from the day's unexpected activities, a wave of sleep washed over her. And yet, she could not rest.

"Good night. Sleep well."

They faded to silence. She could not hear his breathing from the other side of the room. She turned over, away from him. Still, no matter how welcoming that bed was, rest did not take her, She soon turned again. The fire had burned low before she sat up, knowing she would not sleep. She sighed and ran her hand through her hair, scooping back a loose strand that had freed itself from her braid.

"Are you still awake?" Kass murmured.

"I'm sorry. Did I wake you?"

He rolled over and sat up. She had not realised that he had taken his hair out of his customary knot. It hung around his face, messy and tousled. He gave her a lopsided, exhaustion-filled grin. "No. I cannot sleep either."

"We can swap if you like. I don't mind. I'll take the rug. I feel terrible kicking you out of your own bed."

Kass batted a hand at her. "It's not that."

"Then what?"

"Hmm." His look was entirely too suggestive as he dragged his gaze across her. "Suffice to say, I have much to occupy my mind at present."

That, she could relate to. Venya sat up, crossed her legs

under the cover, and placed her hands in her lap. She shrugged. "Then, tell me about it? If neither of us are to sleep, we may as well pass the time."

He eyed her.

"Tell me about you," she clarified. "You are very different to all the stories I have heard."

"I'm not." He snorted.

She frowned. "Yes, you are. I expected some cruel, malevolent sorcerer in a dark keep in the woods, not… you."

"Me?" He arched a brow.

"Yes. You have been nothing but generous. Hospitable, chivalrous, respectful."

"You're going to make me blush," he said sardonically.

"It makes me wonder, is all. You are either a very good liar, or the stories do not hold true." She shifted, stroking the soft coverlet, dropping her gaze from his.

Kass scoffed.

"What?" She looked up again.

"Nothing." He shifted, leaning back onto his hands, legs outstretched, that glorious torso of his on full display. She could not help but stare at him. He was at complete ease in the heart of his home.

"Where did you come by such a terrible reputation?" she dared to ask.

His expression closed, and his jaw clenched. In the dying embers of the fire, his expression looked all the more severe. But she waited. Did not retract her question.

"It was Laurent," he said eventually. He sat up, drew a knee to his chest, and rested his arm upon it. "I was young, barely more than a boy, and extremely foolish. I am fae, you know that." His eyes dropped to the floor. "I thought I was invincible. I was an arrogant dolt."

She waited, barely daring to breathe, not at all daring to

move, as she watched the walls within him crumble between them. She had heard of Laurent in the tales. He was the Destroyer of Laurent, if his reputation were true. A full city. In one night. Gone.

What did he do? Horror lurched through her.

CHAPTER TWENTY-EIGHT

Pity stirred in Venya as Kassimir buried his face in his hands.

"There was a demon. In those days, I did not hunt them—not yet—but I was convinced I could capture one. Harness its power as my own. I released it from its captivity. I was not able to harness it. It broke free and destroyed Laurent.

"Laurent was my home. My family was there. Parents. Cousins Aunts. Uncles. My friends. It was a centre for the arts. The streets were rich with music and murals. It was a jewel of my people. I hear their screams every night. I hear the crackle of the flames devouring Laurent—devouring them all."

Horror swallowed that pity as Venya imagined what he spoke of.

"The demon obliterated every last one."

"But you survived."

"I did," he said, his voice muffled in his hands. He looked up at her, utterly wretched. "The demon would have continued unchecked, devouring a new city every day, had I not found a way to stop it. To contain it."

"How did you do it?" Venya breathed, clutching the blanket in her fists.

"I bound him to my soul."

Her lips parted. That was unheard of.

"Using the power of that destruction—all those deaths in one place, that disturbance to the well of magic—I could think of nothing else to do. I could not contain it. Its prison had been destroyed with the rest of the city and so… I became its prison."

"You?" She looked at him with fresh horror. Now, with deep shadows dancing upon his face from the last of those embers, he looked threatening. Terrifying, even. She shrank back in the bed, keenly aware of just how vulnerable she was. Had she been right to trust him? He had conducted himself nothing but well towards her, but if he held a *demon* inside him…

"Me," he admitted softly, his words bitter with guilt and shame. "It is locked within me—for now. I have borne its torment for centuries. I will not much longer."

He looked so tired as he met her eyes with such an utterly hopeless stare that it tugged at her heart with worry.

"What do you mean?"

"The Darkyn attacks grow each week of late. It means my power fades. It means the time nears when I will no longer be strong enough to keep the demon imprisoned inside me."

"What then?" Her voice was almost silent.

"Then, it will break free. I will be the first of its victims, and then it will be free to cause devastation, the likes of which will make Laurent look like nothing."

"W-when?"

"Starfall."

Now, it made more sense. "That's why you want to marry. It's something to do with averting this."

"Yes."

"How?"

"A fool's hope, perhaps. But I intend to bind it anew. To ensure it does not escape."

"Is it in there—you—now?"

He nodded. "I keep it controlled. Do not fear. You are safe with me. I promise."

She swallowed. Despite the fear lurking in the dark corners of the room, fuelled by night, she did feel safe with him, on an instinctive level she could not explain.

"I am sorry," he whispered. "I did not mean to dupe you. But you see, I am quite desperate."

"I understand." And she did. Sadness was a lake within her heart, burden-filled vessels the only lonely visitors to its shores.

His bed chamber drowned in the weight of their pooling guilt and shame. He dropped his head into his hands again. Venya's chest hurt at the sight of his pain. He seemed so strong, invincible, unruffled in the days she had known him, but now, he seemed utterly undone. Lost.

She slipped from the bed to pad across to him on silent feet. "It was a terrible, terrible mistake."

"It was my fault," came the muffled reply.

She knelt beside him and placed a soft hand on his arm, pulling it away from his face. Then the other. He looked at her with wet eyes. At the sight of them, she could not help but wordlessly pull him into an embrace.

He buried his face into her neck, his nose nestling into her collar bone, and his arms wrapped around her, one hand snaking up her back, the other pulling her waist closer. They locked together in silence, the occasional crack of the fire in the hearth the only sound punctuating the rhythmic thump of his heartbeat pulsing through her from their joined chests.

"I did not mean to upset you," she said into his hair. "I'm sorry." She felt both lighter and heavier for it. Lighter, because she instinctively trusted his words. He perhaps was not the feared, reviled sorcerer from the tales. They had grown all the more wicked in the telling and he had not been there to defend the honour of his reputation.

Yet, he carried the weight of guilt for it. If there was anything she understood, it was that. Guilt had long been her only silent companion throughout the walks of her life. How long had it been his only heavy company in these lonely halls?

"There is nothing for you to be sorry for," he said into her neck, the vibrations of his words against her skin tightening something inside her. "I wish you would stop carrying such guilt, for it is not your fault. You torture yourself for that which is out of your control or responsibility."

"As do you," she rebuked him softly. "You made a terrible, terrible mistake, but is the price worth carrying with you all your days? You may never feel you can make amends for any of it, but if you can stop it coming to pass again. I should think that the best repentance you could embark upon."

Kassimir pulled away from her neck and stared at her, his brow furrowed and his eyes filled with such feeling she could not tear away. Venya's chest heaved under the weight of his attention, the feel of his hands upon her waist through that thin shirt all too sensitive. Her stomach clenched. They were too close. This was too dangerous. She could not enjoy this— this was to be nothing more than an arrangement of convenience and penance—and yet, she wanted to.

Their faces were so close, their breath mingled. "Skies above, I do not know how. You undo me," he said.

His words unravelled her defences. One arm held her tight, winding around her. The other released, and his hand cupped her cheek. Slowly, he drew her closer, until he had to tilt his face to stop their noses from bumping.

Her arms wound tighter around him of their own accord, her hands splaying on his bare back, fingers seeking the dips and peaks of his muscles, the ruptures and rivers of his scars. Now, she could not stop them, even if she wanted to. And the trouble was, she did not. She did not hate him as she was supposed to.

Her breath hitched as their lips threatened to touch and heat pooled in her core at the sensation of his hot breath against her mouth. His eyes were so close she was lost in their swirling gold and silver depths, cast in shadows by the now-dead fire as the last of its light faded.

He was giving her the chance to retreat if she wanted, she realised. Holding himself so perfectly still, their lips a hair away from contact. She did not want to, and in that moment, she cast aside any judgement on herself and closed her eyes, surrendering to his control.

His lips brushed hers. Softly at first. Then, more insistent. That hand upon her cheek wound to the back of her head, pulling her closer. She opened to his sculpted mouth with a moan and he deepened the kiss, teasing her tongue with his. Her back arched, their chests pressing together, and her hands rose to tangle in his hair as he claimed kiss after kiss, until they tore apart, their ragged breathing filling the chamber.

She saw the outline of his heaving chest, the part of his lips, and the solid line of his cheekbone in the last light. Her hands rested on his chest. His at her waist and neck. Her core was on fire, every part of her hypersensitive. When his fingers trembled, she knew he felt the same.

"Venya," he said at the same moment she breathed his name. He moaned softly and dropped his forehead to rest upon her collarbone. "You undo me. I want to… and yet, I cannot."

Relief and dismay mingled. He was right. They should not. They both knew it. It would not fix either of their guilt, only complicate things between them. Even if she would have enjoyed every second of his body.

She wrenched herself away from the temptation of him before she could weaken. Common sense and coldness rushed into the breach.

What were you thinking, Venya?

CHAPTER TWENTY-NINE

Kass lay in the dark, listening to Venya's soft breathing. He had insisted she take the bed, and he had wanted nothing more than to join her, but he knew that way lay only folly and ruin.

He felt like a damn fool for pouring his heart out to her. A damn, infatuated, blind fool. He hated himself more that he held the worst of it back, all whilst allowing himself to enjoy the taste of her. He had not intended to share any of it, but somehow, she opened him up. Tore down his defences. Made him feel as though there was a sliver of hope.

There was not.

She just did not know that yet. He grimaced and shoved his face into the pelt he laid upon, wishing he could scream his rage and fear into it, but he would not wake her for his own pitiful, selfish ends.

That she trusted him enough to sleep so unguardedly whilst he remained so near only cut him up all the more. He wanted to scream at her, too. *Don't trust me!* He wanted nothing more, but he deserved nothing less, for he saw no future in which he did not betray her.

She trusted him not to take advantage of her as she slept. Even though he had not laid another finger upon her and would not without her permission, it still felt like he took horrible advantage of her, though in a different way.

"Lamb to slaughter," crooned the demon, uncurling inside him.

Kass gritted his teeth and rolled onto his back, staring up at the dark ceiling, willing the Darkyn inside him to cease its endless, torturous mutterings. It did not. Every minute of the long night became an eternity as he stared into the darkness —and the darkness stared back, wearing his face.

CHAPTER THIRTY

When Venya awoke—taking a moment to realise with a rush that she was still in Kassimir's bed and wrapped in his sheets and his scent—Kassimir was gone. She rolled over. The other side of the bed remained undisturbed. Memories flooded back, along with that heat rising to her cheeks and sinking to her core. Memories of that kiss. That parting. The mingled regret and relief.

Venya groaned and lay back on her pillow, squeezing her eyes shut. Overnight, things had become significantly more complicated. She forced herself to move, slipping out of bed and clutching his shirt close as she padded to the bathroom. The door was already open, flooding light into the shuttered bedroom and those dark drapes that blocked out all natural light from the chamber. White light, reflected from the fresh snowfall outside.

Venya peered out onto the snow-covered forest, unbroken right to the mountains. She washed in the sink and returned to Kassimir's bedroom. Still no sign of him, but on top of her pile of clothes lay a note.

She scanned it.

Venya, I did not want to wake you. I'll be back. I must finish the hunt. Stay inside. You are safe. Kass.

It was as brusque as he was. She smiled, a warmth stealing through her chest as she held it close. She sighed.

Stop it, Venya. This means nothing. Just a moment of weakness. Remember, he has practically tricked you into marrying him. He has a demon *inside him.* That gave pause to the rose-tinted thoughts.

Venya dressed hurriedly in her clothes, rumpled and soiled as they were, and without a backwards glance, fled Kassimir's chamber. The sooner she was out of there, the better. Her head cleared as she took the stairs to her room. She stripped again and slipped on the dove grey dress she had rejected the previous day. Dresses were not her style, but it was clean and did not smell of *him* at least.

She ventured to the dining room, where a single breakfast awaited her—and Pata. That day, left to her own devices, she and Pata wandered the halls, exploring the castle and conversing. The construct had been with Kassimir for several hundred years—she marvelled at that alone—and had plenty of interesting tales to tell about his master, though he refused to share any of the juicy ones. Their laughter echoed down the halls as he recounted how he had once rescued Kass after he had fallen in a river half drunk and required the big cat to drag him out.

After a sedate lunch, Venya ended up in the libraries, of course, and lost her afternoon curled up on one of the couches in the drawing room, reading through a stack of titles she had pulled from the main reading room. She glanced up every now and then. She had chosen the couch next to the window for a reason. It overlooked the main courtyard. There was no sign of Kassimir.

CHAPTER THIRTY-ONE

Kass had to tear himself away that morning, else he never would have left. It had stirred something deep within him to wake up to Venya stretched out sleeping in his bed, the covers gathered around her waist, his own shirt covering her body, and her braid having escaped so her raven hair fanned across his pillows.

He had longed to run his fingers through it and give her a most pleasant waking to continue what they had started the night before, but he did not deserve that, and she did not want it. They had stopped for precisely that reason. So, he had torn himself away, given himself a rough wash in the snow outside, rubbing himself down with it and hoping to gain some of his head back in the process. Then, he had charged into the forest, leaving her a note that said absolutely nothing about his damned feelings.

He was half in the business of a hunt, and half-avoiding the guilt that nipped at his heels. He could not outrun it, no matter how far and fast he shifted through shadow and wind. But, as he latched onto the train of the Darkyn that had eluded him, he did, at least, have a worthy distraction from the writhing internal turmoil. Part of him dared not face her again.

CHAPTER THIRTY-TWO

"*H*e returns." Pata's solemn voice started Venya from her reading. The big cat poked his head around the drawing room door.

She blinked and frowned. *When did it get dark?* "Is everything alright?"

"Hmm. He's limping. So probably not."

With a sharp intake of breath, Venya abandoned the book on the cushion beside her and stood. "Take me to him."

Pata did not object to the order, though his unblinking green-eyed glare bored into her for a second longer than was necessary.

Venya followed him to… Her heart rose and sank. Kassimir's bedchamber. She slipped inside after the big cat, who yowled to make their presence known. It was empty, but the bathroom was illuminated.

"Hide anything you do not wish to be seen, a fair maiden approaches and I do not wish her eyes to be sullied by anything indecent, Kass."

Only a grunt answered them.

"No sarcasm? That's a bad sign." Pata padded to the bathroom.

Venya followed and entered. "Kassimir!" He was slumped beside the giant bath, his hair a loose tangle. She rushed to him and dropped to her knees beside him. "Are you well? What has happened? You're so pale."

He raised his head to look her in the eye—he was dog-tired, his eyes hazy and unfocused. "Pata, I don't know how but please, will you bring something for him to eat? He'll be famished." From the rumblings of her own stomach, it was dinnertime, but she could wait.

Pata turned and sauntered out. "Seeing as you asked so nicely."

Venya sighed and turned to Kass. "What scrape did you get yourself in?"

"A necessary one," he croaked.

"Backchat," she remarked, arching a brow. "You can't be dying, then."

He managed a small grin at that.

"Are you hurt?"

He gestured to his chest, grimaced, and dropped his hand.

"I'm going to need to get this off to see the extent." Venya's lips thinned. A dark stain spread through his surcoat, and the fabric was ripped to shreds. She clicked her tongue. The garment was ruined regardless. It would hurt too much to try and take it off, so she ripped it from him.

"Tearing my clothes off? Control yourself…"

"You wish." She sniffed. His comment had been weak, filled with none of his usual spirit—that scared her. What had he done? She peeled the fabric away carefully, grimacing as he winced and hissed a sharp intake of breath.

His chest was *ruined*. Much like Imperion's, it had been torn by huge claws, only unlike the construct's, Kassimir's chest bled. She swallowed and steeled herself. Blood did not bother her. She had seen plenty over the years—her own and others'—and she was a female, for heaven's sake. It came with every moon. Her head switched into 'pragmatic mode.'

"I'll work as quickly as I can. I'm sorry if this hurts. I'll do my best."

His only answer was a grimace.

Venya placed her splayed fingers on his chest, either side of those gaping wounds, her movements precise and careful.

Kassimir bit down on a moan that she felt bubble from the depths of his chest into her fingertips.

She did not respond. This held none of the emotion of the prior night. Now, anxiety laced the edge of her concentration and there was absolutely no swooping in her stomach. She breathed deep, in and out, slowing her heart rate down. This always worked better if she was clear-headed and calm.

Then, she opened her connection to the wellspring of magic and pulled it forth, channelling it through her fingers, using herself as the conduit, and pushing its healing power into him. It was like clay in her hands, malleable and soft. It allowed her to push it into muscle groups and knit the fibres back together, tease it across the skin to repair the sundered flesh, and seek out those broken blood vessels—none serious, thankfully—to re-join them. Pressure built in her forehead with the weight of concentration, holding all those different elements of his body together, directing the flow of magic to where it was most needed, and making sure she had the right amount of power.

Kassimir hissed. "That tickles," he said through clenched teeth.

"It could be worse!" She clenched her eyes shut, finding the very last of the fissure in his chest and sealing it. It had been a flesh wound—a nasty one—but nothing more serious, thank goodness. She kept up the flow of magic just a tad longer than she needed, using it to replenish his energy, but now she was spent.

She could tell he needed it from the sigh of relief that escaped him.

Venya opened her eyes. "Better?"

"Much."

"'Thank you' are the words you're looking for," Pata said, sauntering in, a napkin clenched in his jaws.

"Thank you," said Kass, locking eyes with Venya.

Now, crisis averted, something did flutter deep in her stomach at the way he spoke only to her, as though the rest of the world did not matter.

Pata spat the napkin on the floor and a lump of cheese, ham, and bread roll spilled out. "I meant thank me! I don't know if you appreciate how difficult that was without opposing thumbs, you cretin."

Kass glared at him. "Get out, you oversized cat. My head is pounding, and I have no inclination to put up with your attitude tonight."

Pata hissed at him. "Ungrateful wretch." Nevertheless, he stalked out, his tail and head held high.

Kass rested his head back on the side of the bath with a *thump*.

Venya admired her handiwork. Pink and puckered, his chest was not a pretty sight, but it was healed, with no lasting damage. That would fade in time, or perhaps leave more scars. Her attention traced over the rest of his torso. Well-lit for the first time, now she viewed all his scars in full, stark glory.

"Are they burns?" she whispered, gaping at him.

Kassimir's throat bobbed. "Yes. I was not uninjured in Laurent. I went into the fires to try and find anyone to save."

She bit down on more questions. "You need sleep. Let me help you." She stood and offered him a hand.

"I need a wash." Kass took a sniff of his armpit and groaned. He struggled to his feet and twisted over the bath. "Though I appreciate the cat's effort, I need more than a lump of hard cheese to see me through. Have you eaten?"

"No."

"In that case, please, would you fetch us both something? There'll be something in the pantry, in the kitchens."

"Of course." She turned. That solved two problems: her stomach's complete mutiny and avoiding absolutely any temptation around Kassimir.

"Venya."

She turned on the threshold.

He watched her, dark shadows under his eyes, and his large form crumpled, leaning on the bath rim. "Thank you."

She swallowed, nodded, and left.

CHAPTER THIRTY-THREE

When she returned, the bath was full, and from the sound of sloshing water, he was in it. She ate her plate of food—cold meats, potatoes, and vegetables—as she waited. Soon, he emerged. She averted her gaze as he slipped on some trousers and then offered him his plate.

He groaned with delight as the first morsel hit his tongue. "Blessed food." She sat upon the ottoman to eat, cross-legged, and he settled on the edge of the bed nearby.

When they had finished, he took her plate silently and left them both on the mantel. He grimaced at the movement. She was with him in a flash.

"Are you alright? Is it hurting?" *Did I miss something?* There had been darkness in the wound, a resistance to her healing—some remnant of the Darkyn's attack, for their very essence was darkness—but she thought she had removed the last of it. Perhaps…

"I'm fine." He smiled tightly.

She paused before him, her fingers already outstretched to examine that wound, moving without thought. She snatched her hands back. "Of course."

He smiled a tired, warm smile. "It tugs. Feels somewhat unpleasant. I'll survive."

"Good." She stifled a yawn. "I'd best let you get some rest." She brushed past him to leave, but he caught her wrist, tugging her back.

"Please don't." His head bent low, his mouth near her ear.

"Kassimir?" She froze at the feeling of his breath grazing her neck.

"Please don't leave me." His grip softened, his hand gliding down her arm, that touch now eliciting sparks of an entirely non-magical nature across her skin.

Venya swallowed, her breath fluttering across her lips as she closed her eyes. This was dangerous. Had she not only that morning resolved there would be no more of this?

"I ask for nothing other than your company. I do not wish to be alone tonight. Facing those demons took much from me. I cannot face the darkness too. Stay with me… I beg you."

"Nothing but my company?" she asked, steeling herself. Willing away the swoop low in her stomach that wanted *more*.

"Just that."

Against her better judgement, Venya turned slowly towards him. "You must take the bed tonight. I insist." She gave him a look that brooked no argument and hoped that not a single shred of desire leaked out.

"I cannot see you on the floor."

"What other solution would you have?"

Something ticked in his jaw. "Join me," he said, his voice low.

"I beg your pardon?" The words burst out of her.

"I promise I will not lay a finger upon you. I shall never touch you unless you ask for it. My body still aches from last night and I confess, I have no desire to repeat a night on the hearth. I am dead upon my feet. But, I will not see you sleep on the floor all for my weak desperation."

Say no. This is a mistake. "If you insist. I shall hold you to your word."

She saw the relief as he dragged a palm over his face. *What has him in such a state that he is so desperate for company?* She had not pegged him for one afraid of the dark—this was something deeper. Something she did not yet understand.

"You owe me for this," she said slyly.

Smiling faintly, he inclined his head and shuffled to the bed. He peeled the cover back and lowered himself into bed with more than one wince.

She retreated to the bathroom to change into one of his shirts to sleep in again, because she did not know how else to deal with the exceptional situation she now found herself in. Sharing the bed of Kassimir the Dark. Willingly. He who had promised not to touch her unless she asked… but damned be him, she wanted to. Who would this be a greater test for? Given the previous night's activity, he seemed just as interested as her. This was a mess, alright.

She returned and slipped into the bed, keeping a distance between them. He shuffled right to his edge. "Shall we build a wall between us, milady?"

She could not help but smile at that as she lay on her side facing him. *I want nothing less…*

He reclined and stared up at the ceiling. "You smile, but you do not answer me." He trailed off for a moment. "Thank you for humouring me. I know you did not wish to be here— for any of this to happen—but for what it is worth, I am most glad you came, Venya."

She remained silent.

He turned to her. The lights remained illuminated, and he seemed to have no inclination to darken the room. She supposed that was something to do with whatever this all was.

His voice was so quiet, she had to lean a little closer to hear him. "You give me hope when I had none. Perhaps, like Arielle rescued Leander, you will rescue me. A fool can hope." He shot her a wry smile.

A lump formed in her throat. "I see you read the more romantic translation. Did you not know of the original?"

He furrowed a brow. "That is the original."

"No. It's not. The original is older still, passed down only by oral storytelling. No written records survived, though they were later recorded. The modern tale—the popular one—tells of how they rescued each other and Arielle used her magic to ascend them both to the Court of Stars in the Sky Kingdom."

Venya shook her head. "I admit I was sad to find that was not the original tale. No. The original tale is sadder. Darker. Leander could not rescue Arielle from her captor. He died, painfully and brutally, in the attempt. When her captor paraded his broken body before her, it is said she died of a broken heart. In dying, they both did escape to a realm where none could follow. But that realm was not the kingdom of the stars high above. It was death."

At that last word, she saw him flinch. Watched him crumple before her.

"Kassimir?" She did not understand. "What's wrong?"

He only clenched his jaw and shook his head, turning to stare at the ceiling once more. "I'm fine."

"Is it your wound?"

"No."

"It's just a story."

"I said I'm *fine*!"

CHAPTER THIRTY-FOUR

enya recoiled from that, visibly hurt. Kass hated himself even more for causing it. So much hurt he would cause her, damn him. But this... She did not deserve it. He had asked her to stay. She was so kind, of course she had. It was selfish of him. He was nothing but a coward.

When he faced the Darkyn, his nightmares were always worse. So depleted, he could not face them alone. Not tonight. With her there, her presence felt like a talisman of hope, a shield to hide behind. He needed that desperately— some help to find his courage where there was none.

It felt so good to have her close, even though she had turned her back on him and did not yet sleep. He heard as much from her breathing. But the silence had stretched too long. He could not apologise now.

He cursed himself silently.

"Yes, you are a coward, aren't you?" the demon agreed. He felt the disembodied smile within him.

Leave me be, Ozul. Please.

Ozul only cackled. Of course, if he asked it for such a

boon, it would deliver doubly the opposite. He felt its claws sink dark talons into the deepest recesses of his mind. He was tired. So tired.

He struggled against it, exhaustion forcing him to succumb to sleep. Raggedly, he held on. He would not cede. Could not. He could not face the nightmares again. The terror and guilt, the fear and shame of what had passed that night in Laurent. Watching his loved ones die. Surging into the flames and finding nothing but death.

The demon had spared him only to watch, to revel in his pain. He had exploited that one minor flaw to capture it, and now, in repayment, it would never let him forget. Night after night, those nightmares grew worse. Tonight… *Please let me have some reprieve.*

"I will make you watch whilst I feast upon her heart, and then I shall tear yours to shreds." The demon dragged him into its realm and did not let go.

CHAPTER THIRTY-FIVE

It was the cold that woke Venya. A creeping chill that stole the very breath from her lungs. She stirred. Her feet were blocks of ice. Why was it so cold all of a sudden? The castle was heated by fire and magic. She had not been cold there yet.

She blinked the sleep away from her eyes, and froze.

The lamps were still lit. And with them, she beheld the full terror of a creature of pure darkness which crouched atop Kassimir beside her in the bed.

Kassimir's spine arched, throwing his head back into the pillow and thrusting his chest up into the air to an inhuman degree. The creature had folded its unnatural body small, but its limbs were far longer than hers, longer even than Kassimir's. Atop the knobble of every vertebra was a vicious spike.

Venya did not dare draw breath. Pure malevolence rolled from this creature in waves that threatened to make her gag. And that unnatural cold seeped from it—or from Kassimir, she could not tell. Her eyes darted to him. His olive skin was pale. Hoarfrost sparkled upon his loose hair and crusted his eyelashes.

Was he… *dead?* She could barely dare to think it.

As she watched, it lowered its terrible head to Kassimir's face. It had an elongated snout and a great maw so wide it stretched two hand spans. It opened that jaw to reveal cruelly pointed teeth formed from shards of darkness. This whole being seemed made of pure night, but not the gentle good kind, but the night of crushing, rending nightmares. Its pure black eyes shone molten in the lamplight as it regarded its prey.

Of two things, Venya was certain.

This was a demon.

And if she was not careful, they were both dead.

She took a sharp breath.

And the demon's attention snapped to her. It was an arm's length away.

Lightning fear lanced through her veins, giving her the courage to move. She thrust the covers into its face and rolled off the bed, landing in a crouch. She dived to the foot of the bed where the ottoman gave some small barrier between her and the *thing* and snatched Kassimir's dark dagger from atop the pile of clothes there.

It launched itself at her, its tail of smoke and shadow lashing behind it. Venya threw herself to one side, that dagger sweeping out in a giant cutting arc behind her.

The demon shrieked in such an unearthly tone it shattered her hearing. She had caught it a glancing blow upon the arm. It did not bleed, but smoke leached from it in great wafts that choked her with their acidic smoky tang. Every part of her singing with terror and desperation, she darted forward as it turned, dragging that blade across its abdomen in a great slicing cut that had its dark innards spilling forth.

She jumped onto the ottoman and turned to face it, emboldened—and had to dive onto the bed to avoid its scything hooked claws.

She bounced into Kassimir. "Wake up, Kass!" she screamed, slapping him across the face—he felt freezing to the touch. He did not move.

Two great arms of darkness wrapped around her waist and pulled her backwards off the bed. Through the light shirt, its touch both burned and froze her. She struggled, shrieking, but its grip only intensified, and a sibilant hiss burst from it.

"Hello, Venya, ssssso niccce to meet you at lassssst."

Venya still held the dagger. She flipped the hilt in her hand and rammed it back to one side of her waist. It thudded into something solid.

Those arms loosened at once. Venya dropped to the ground and whirled around. She had to scramble back to avoid its flailing claws. In its midriff, darkness oozed out in thick glugs, singeing the carpet where it fell.

A groan behind her.

Venya turned to see Kass rolling onto his side. She rushed to him. "Kass, wake up, please. There's a demon!" She stood, brandishing that dagger as the demon stalked closer. It was less cocky now, remaining at a distance, its gleaming, bulbous eyes fixed upon that blade in her outstretched hand. But it circled still, and did not retreat. It had not given up the hunt.

Kass sat up. Staggered to his feet.

"Kass?"

"Oh Kasssssssimir…" the demon crooned.

Kass's attention snapped to it. Venya rushed to support him, shrugging one of his arms around her shoulders, leaving her knife arm free.

"I wassss enjoying our little nightmare, were you? And then, I had the mosssst unwelcome interruption." The demon's head cocked to an unnatural angle as it regarded Venya. "Ssssuch a pleasure to meet your *intended*."

"Not another word!" Kass barked, standing tall, even though his breath shuddered through his chest and he wore a grimace of such tight pain that Venya knew he struggled.

"I will enjoy devouring her, oh yesssss." It inched forward. Venya recognised the predatory crouch it lowered into. It would pounce and overwhelm both of them.

Kass thrust her behind him. "Touch her and I will end you!" he roared, and from nowhere, the lights flared to such bright extremes that Venya was forced to throw an arm up to cover her eyes.

The demon fell back, shrieking, and diminished before her eyes into something smaller and less corporeal, trying to escape the light by folding into a corner, but to no avail.

"Get down," Kass ground out, and Venya dropped to a knee. He swiped the dagger from her and stalked towards the demon. The dagger flashed from his hand and sliced through the air.

She felt the rumble of his magic growing. The demon shrieked and tried to find a way out through cracks in the wall, but that dagger pinned it in place.

Smaller and smaller the darkness became, writhing around that blade. It folded inwards until the very last wisp of shadow had vanished, leaving only the stench of ash and sulphur upon the air, burned patches of carpet, and complete pandemonium behind it.

CHAPTER THIRTY-SIX

"Is it dead?" Venya asked, rising to her feet. Kass retrieved his dagger from the wall and turned to her. He felt that angry beast writhing inside him, furious at being subdued. Dizziness swelled, and he braced a hand against the wall.

"No. It is contained for now. It cannot stand the blade—it is made to repel the Darkyn." He staggered over to her. "Are you well? It did not hurt you?"

She brushed him off, though she was pale. "I'm fine. I'm more worried about you. You look like death warmed up."

"Thanks for noticing," he said dryly. He ran a hand through his hair. It was slightly damp from where the hoar-frost had melted.

"What happened?" Her words were quiet, and she watched him solemnly now. She deserved some answers.

"I am depleted after the past few days. When I am weaker, he can escape more easily. We are still tied together. That does not change. However, I find it harder to keep him from the surface. The nightmares are worse, and in the worst of them, he grows strong enough to find a corporeal form."

She eyed him critically. "Will it return?"

"Tonight, no. It has retreated to nurse the wounds you gave it." *For now.* He sank onto the bed. This was a war with an inexorable outcome. His total loss.

She perched next to him. "Talk to me."

Kass shook his head. What could he say? "I cannot defeat this," he said eventually, his voice low. It was painful to give voice to his deepest fear.

"Yes, you can. *We* can." She reached out to clasp his hand. Hers felt so warm on his, still cold from the demon's power. He heard the kernel of determination in her voice, but he could not bring himself to hope.

"I cannot carve this monstrosity from within me."

"Cannot?"

"It can be done," he amended. "This blade it capable of such things. However, I can not accomplish it alone." And that had been the crux of his problem.

"I've been thinking..." she said slowly. "You create grimoires and I contain them."

He tilted his head at her, raising an eyebrow. Waiting.

"I have seen grimoires before. Ones that hold demons. Multiple demons and spirits, in fact. Creature compendiums containing all the beings they describe. Marvellous things. Though slightly terrifying." She half-grimaced, half-smiled. "Well, what if you could create a grimoire to hold this demon? If we could cleave it from your soul, then you could bind it into the grimoire, and I could contain it so that it cannot escape."

He gaped at her. Somehow, she made it sound so simple. It could not be... could it?

"Well? Is that possible?" Her hand loosened on his.

Something like excitement trickled through him. He needed to think on it more but...

"Yes. There is every possibility. This blade can cleave the demon from my soul, but I would need assistance to bind it too whilst I am vulnerable."

He had never thought of it like that before. It seemed quite obvious now that she had said it. He had never considered trying to separate the demon and binding it into a new form. For that, he would need help to cut the demon from his soul and force the demon into a new prison, and that was why he had never considered it, because who would help him?

"I will help you."

He took her hands in his, squeezing them, as that excitement mounted, and with it, surged hope. "You are *brilliant*," he said.

Her answering shy smile lit him up.

Gods, he had been foolish to believe in the pull of some old fairy tale. Starfall. He had misunderstood it all these years, but maybe there was still hope of surviving this calamity.

"I should not have asked you to marry me," he said. "It was desperation, nothing more."

"It was the price you demanded for my mother's cure, and I accepted it of my own free will." Her voice was steady, but that smile leached away and her shoulders drooped. Her gaze fell.

"Neither of us want it. Not truly. I hoped that it would bring some magic to release this demon's hold upon me, for I had little other hope to believe in. And you simply sought a cure for your mother. Let us end this foolishness."

"You do not want to marry me?" She sounded reproachful. Hurt. Confused. He felt much the same.

Kass swallowed. This was it. A moment to choose—to play it safe or stick his neck beyond the parapet.

He pivoted and dropped to a knee before her, still clasping her hand in his. She met his gaze.

"Neither of us wants an arranged marriage," he said carefully. He closed his eyes, trying to find the words, then met her violet eyes once more.

"I want you, Venya. I should not, and *you* should not, and yet I cannot keep myself away from you. I want you to stay. Not because we made a bargain, an arrangement of desperation. I helped you and your mother, and I offer that to you freely now. I would ask you to help me defeat this wretched demon, but I will not extort you to do so. If you choose to stay, that is your choice. I can only ask. As for our arrangement… I release you from it."

He could only hope that she would not take that freedom and run. That she would choose to stay. He watched a flicker of emotions betray her inner turmoil.

"We will no longer be obligated to marry?"

He shook his head. "I only ask—beg—you to stay once the construct returns with proof of your mother's healing, but only if you want to. I will not force you." His shoulders sagged. She was going to reject him and leave. Of course she would. She had everything she came for; a cure for her mother and an offer of freedom, no conditions attached.

His feelings did not matter to her. And he could barely admit to himself that she was the dawn that brought a lifeline of hope that he had needed for so long. She made him forget about the guilt, the pain, and the shame. She made him forget about his impending death. She made him feel as though there might be a chance to thwart it. He had already written off his original plan. He could not sacrifice her. Ever. There would have to be another way and, brilliant female that she was, she seemed to have found one.

She swallowed. "I should like to stay," she admitted in a whisper.

CHAPTER THIRTY-SEVEN

With Kassimir's chamber ruined, Venya retired to her tower room. It felt strangely foreign already. He had declared he would not sleep again and would be busy in his workshop working on her idea. Sleep did not find her either.

They were not to be married anymore. Venya was not quite sure how to feel about that. Relief in part, yes. She had never wanted to marry, not truly. That sense of feeling trapped and pressured had eased immediately. But something more turbulent ran as an undercurrent too—a tinge of disappointment that they were ended before they had ever really begun.

She found Kassimir attractive. Wanted him more than she ought to. He was far from the hateful sorcerer she had envisioned. She felt as though he had allowed her a window into his very soul, and what she had found there was a kindred spirit that called to her on a deeper level than anyone else she had met, despite their many and varied differences.

That pulled her in a different direction, away from the guilt and worry that usually influenced everything she did.

Her mother's health was taken care of—thanks to Kassimir—and with that, her burden eased. A part of her dared to dream as she lay in her bed, tossing and turning.

Perhaps I could pursue something with him purely for the sense of my own enjoyment. It was such a foreign concept that it made her shiver with the fear that it aroused. Pleasure was something that she shied away from, so certain was she that she did not deserve it.

Soon, she gave up on rest and slipped down to his workshop to join him, hooking his cloak from the peg and wrapping it around herself.

He gave her a slow, appreciative smile as she entered, one that made her warm inside, and beckoned her over. He wore a loose shirt and informal breeches. They were smeared with dirt and grease, and his sleeves were rolled all the way up to his elbows. "You could not sleep either?"

"No." She gave him a tired smile. He cocked his head, giving her an evaluative look, and then set his tool down decidedly.

"You know? We have time yet before Starfall, and my construct will return with word from your homelands. Our time so far together has been marred by misfortune." He grimaced. "To hells with it."

Something flipped in her stomach as he stalked towards her with a glint of mischief in his eyes—even though dark shadows still hung beneath those eyes, betraying his exhaustion. She stared up at him as he stood before her.

"How would you like to visit a special place? One I have never taken anyone before."

She frowned. *What does that even mean?*

"Do you trust me?" He held out a hand to her. An open offer.

Her lips parted. *Yes.* She took his hand, and he pulled her into wind and shadow.

A second later and they were outside. She pulled the cloak tight about her as her feet sank into deep snow.

Kassimir threw back his head and laughed as she squawked with surprise and nearly lost her balance. He placed those giant hands of his on her waist and pulled her out of the drift, standing her on a step next to him. She was too busy gawking at what lay behind him to object to his enjoyment of her embarrassment.

She swept her gaze across the space. A clearing in the forest, ringed by snow-laden trees. Soaring so high above that she had to crane her neck were peaks, their summits lost to her perspective from their flanks. It was not those that captured the bulk of her attention, though.

That snagged on the cabin nestled upon the mountainside at the top of the half-dozen steps they stood at the foot of.

"What is this place?" she asked, her gaze roving over it all—the log walls, the shuttered windows, the snow-laden roof.

"This is my haven." She took the hand he offered and allowed him to lead her up the steps. "This is where I come when I need respite from it all. It is warded to the high hilt—none but I can tread here, and the Darkyn have no way to enter. Here, I am safe. Here, I am free."

He dropped her hand to unbar the door, lifting away a giant length of wood from two slots. Then, with a palm pressed on the door, it silently opened. She followed him over the threshold. It was cold and dark inside, but only for a moment. With their entrance, faelights illuminated, and across the space in a hearth of giant stones, a fire flickered to life, catching tinder and kindling and licking at the larger logs waiting to catch.

Warmth and light flooded the space in moments,

augmented by the welcome rush of magic. Kassimir slipped the cloak from Venya's shoulders. She drifted around the space as he unshuttered the windows, allowing the pale winter light to filter through the glass. In the main room, an open-plan space, was a lounge area before the hearth with a comfortable well-worn couch and chairs, a dining area with a small table and two benches, and a kitchen area with a window looking out onto a cliff face.

Stairs led up to a second level, with two bedrooms under the eaves and a bathroom. Venya jumped as Kassimir's voice emanated directly behind her. How had he followed her so quietly?

"This place has the best water pressure. Direct from the glaciers. The hot water is piped from hot springs deep underground."

She eyed the bathtub. *I'll be enjoying that later.*

The smaller of the bedrooms, next to the bathroom, was a single, its window overlooking the cliff too. Like the kitchen, it was at the back of the property. The front bedroom held a large, king-size bed, and more impressively, full-height glass doors leading out onto a wood-railed balcony. Venya peered out. Uninterrupted views of the valleys below including…

"Is that your castle?" She frowned, pointing at the tiny turret in the distance.

"It is indeed."

Venya swallowed. "Why did you bring me here?"

"Why did you come?"

Venya squeezed her eyes shut. *Because I'm tired of punishing myself all the time. Because for once, I just want to enjoy the moment.*

"What aren't you saying?" he asked softly. He prised her hands away from her face, brushed her hair back, and tipped her chin up with a forefinger and thumb to force her to meet his gaze. "You don't have to hold back. Not with me. I know what's going on in there."

"You do?" He was so close. Her chest tightened.

"I do. I guarantee it is the same argument I'm having with myself right now. You can't let your guard down." He leaned in to brush a kiss across her temple. "You cannot let that tight control you keep like a constant leash upon yourself unravel." He brushed a knuckle down her cheek and she leaned into his touch. "No matter how much you want to." He lowered his lips to hers. "And I know you want to—else you would not have come."

He was right. It was not so terrible to enjoy this—whatever it was—for whatever it was worth. For once, she would do something for herself. Her breath shuddered against his lips and her eyes slipped closed.

His words vibrated against her lips. "Let yourself be, for once, Venya. You are *glorious*. Let me worship you. Here, there are no responsibilities. No obligations. Just you and I— and this."

She opened to his kiss, allowing every tension-filled muscle to melt.

THEY SPENT the rest of the day entangled. Venya had never had such a day devoted to nothing but pleasure—nor anyone so intent on delivering it to her. By the time sunset came, they were ravenous for food, their appetite for each other slaked—for now. Kass cooked dinner and they ate, sitting side by side at the table, before enjoying some dessert on the pelt before the fire and then retreating upstairs.

At last, when the stars were high, they were too tired to continue. Kass pulled Venya against him and there she nestled, pressed up against his chest, and fell asleep, content and at peace.

He woke her with a kiss and breakfast in bed, and it was with reluctance that they returned to the castle that lunchtime.

Venya did not want to leave that sanctuary of peace. Not to return to the gritty reality of what awaited them—their looming deadlines. Hers to hear of her mother's saved health. His to find a way out of his impossible and deadly situation. Her shoulders felt heavier with responsibility the moment he pulled them both from shadow and ether into the courtyard. That sense of ease, that relief from guilt, already faded.

CHAPTER THIRTY-EIGHT

Venya buried herself in research whilst Kass repaired his room after the demon attack. Now they had returned, the press of time had anxiety roiling in her. They had mere days to save Kass from his fate. She had to ensure that the bindings she made for the grimoire—physical chains imbued with magic and spell work to seal the demon inside an enchantment—were infallible. It was the only chance they stood. If they could even separate the denizen from Kass's soul. Venya shivered at that thought. That was an entirely different problem, and one outside her remit.

Her thoughts churned as she read in the library, the vivid memories from their time in the cabin taunting her. It seemed so surreal, like a dream and nothing more. She wondered if it was. Her head dropped into her hands and she rubbed the tiredness away from her eyes. Now that they had returned to the castle, doubt wormed its way inside her.

Is he just using me for his own ends? Things like... well, what had happened in that cabin, simply did not happen to her.

Much as she thought she was quite fine with the breaking of their arrangement, she had to admit, something about it still stung, niggling at her. She had thought it was because he respected her enough to give her the freedom of choice. Was it?

Or is it because he doesn't want you? Because he wanted to use you instead?

Her cheeks burned when she thought of what they had done in that cabin. She had let her self-control slip, lost in the heat of those moments and captured by his charm.

She growled and shoved her doubts away and turned the page so fiercely it almost ripped. *Come on. Concentrate.*

It took all day for Kass to repair the damage caused by the demon, not to mention rid his bedroom of that terrible lingering stench. As he worked, Pata reported that there had been three more demon incursions on the fringes of his territory. It was not the news he wanted to hear.

Like called to like.

The ascent of the demon's power within him was a beacon to its kin. Until he found some way to contain or destroy it, the Darkyn would keep coming until his lands were overwhelmed. Here in the wilds, he was the only bastion standing against them. He had no army, save for the constructs he had made, and they were too few, and not powerful enough to withstand the onslaught of the coming darkness.

It was enough to make him despair.

The demon added to his turmoil, crooning darkness in his mind all day and all night until he was so ground down, he could not remember the day of the week. With dogged determination, Kass threw himself into understanding how to sever the demon from his soul and crafting the perfect grimoire to hold it.

CHAPTER THIRTY-NINE

Venya had barely seen Kass for days. It was a stark contrast to the cabin; there, they had not been parted for more than a few minutes. Now, she was lucky to see him for a few scant moments in the dining room, if he even remembered to eat. According to Pata, he took his meals in the workshop now.

She wanted to storm down there and confront him, but she did not want to know the answer. He had pulled away from her. It was all the proof she needed to validate her worries. The cabin had been nothing but a distraction for both of them. Letting off steam. He did not truly want her. In response, her own stubbornness rose. She would not go to him.

All I need is news of Mother. She needed to hold on for just a little longer, for that construct to arrive any day with proof of her mother's rejuvenated health, and then she would be free to leave. There was no arranged marriage anymore. No reason to stay. No "them."

I don't want him. I don't need him. She tried to convince herself as she pored over text after text, pulling details for her part in their task. *It was an indulgence. A dream. Nothing more, Venya. You just need to help Kass find a solution to his own mess, because it's the right thing to do, and then you can leave.*

She hated how much that hurt. The thought had her gritting her teeth. She scrunched her eyes shut and sunk into the flow of magic to escape the complexity of her emotions. Instead, she focused on the complicated magic she had to employ. It was painstaking, precise work to craft the restraints she needed for this grimoire. From Kass and her research, she knew that like called to like—and opposites repelled. The demons, the Darkyn, were attracted to each other, so to bind it, she would have to cage it inside light.

They were almost finished. Delicate chains of pure light. They looked like light-filled crystals, fragile and precious, but they were as strong as they needed to be. She set to crafting the padlock to match. That would see the demon contained and bound. *If*—and that was the crucial question—Kassimir could cleave the demon from his soul, she could help him bind it.

CHAPTER FORTY

Kass dragged a hand across his face, trying to rub some life into his eyes. It did not work. He was exhausted. Another day had passed inexplicably quickly. It was dark. He had forgotten to eat again and his head swam. He dropped his face into his hands and let out a frustrated growl.

What am I missing?

His research had yielded some answers, but it still felt terrifyingly inadequate. Starfall loomed. So did the day of his death—and hers, if she remained close to him. That was an entirely new level of fear he was not comfortable shouldering.

He dragged himself away from his workbench, tatters of magic spread about the space, half-done experimentations. Nothing had gone far enough to be complete. He needed sleep, food, and her, but she had not returned to his bed. That stung too. He thought they had something between them, but upon their return to the castle, it had soured in an instant. He did not have the mental space to figure out why.

Kass stumbled to bed and collapsed, fully clothed and

stinking, on top of the covers. He was snoring moments later —but no dreamless slumber came to him. Instead, that vicious demon rose and sank its claws in again.

This was another reason he worked so hard and so long. Because now, there was a new nightmare. One more vivid and awful than any that had come before. Now, he faced his worst fear.

Paralysed, Kass could do nothing but lay there and witness as he dragged Venya to a stone altar under the mountains, in dark caves filled with swirling whorls of text written in a savage tongue. There, he shackled her to the table, bruising her pale flesh upon the hard stone as she struggled against him, screaming and crying and lashing out, her fists peppering his chest like rain. And yet, inexorably, he held her down and restrained her.

He tried to pull away. Tried to stop his dream-self from undertaking what he knew would come next, because this was the third night he had witnessed it. He had not managed to drag his awareness away yet. The demon held it there, tearing his emotions to shreds with its violent promises.

And so, Kass could do nothing but watch as he drew that dark dagger of his—the shadow blade that had the power to cleave that accursed creature from him, if he had the strength, but the one that fed it too—and watched as his own hand plunged that knife into her chest. Ozul forced him to watch the shock and pain and betrayal widen her eyes before the life faded from them, sucked out like marrow from a bone by that hateful denizen inside him.

"No!" he screamed, but it was silent and faded into the void, dampened by the demon that delighted in his growing hopelessness and terror.

CHAPTER FORTY-ONE

It was late when Venya retreated from the library, the halls dark and silent. Pata met her partway, his yawning shadow giving her a fright before he rounded the corner and skidded to a halt in front of her.

"Where is Kass?" She could not help but ask. Days now, and she had barely seen him. Did he hold her in such low regard, after all? No matter how much she had tried to convince herself this was entirely superficial and worth nothing, that still stung. That she had misread the situation so much.

"I need your help," Pata said, lashing his tail. He nudged Venya's thigh with his head. "Come. It's a nightmare. A bad one. I fear for him." He was off before Venya could respond.

She sprinted after him, her heart lurching. *Have we run out of time already?* It was not yet Starfall. That was *today*, she realised with a thundering of her heartbeat as it escalated with the fear of that realisation. The clock in the hallway had passed midnight.

They had run out of time. Just one more cycle of the

clock and it would all be over. They had until midnight. If Kass's time had not already expired.

She crashed into his bedroom a second behind Pata. Once more, that demon spread atop him, crouched over his chest.

Its tail lashed possessively, and its attention whipped to them. It hissed—and Pata responded likewise, not pausing as he leapt onto the demon, bowling it off his master.

They tangled on the floor, darkness shredding and golden sparks flying as they fought.

Kass awoke with a gasp, sitting bolt upright. He surveyed the room with wild eyes, taking in the carnage.

Pata yowled and flew across the room, striking the chimney with a thud and falling to the hearth. He rose, growling. The demon advanced upon Kass, pushing him down onto the bed. Kass grasped the dagger from his bedside table and brandished it, forcing the demon to scramble back. Kass struggled off the bed, placing himself between Venya and the demon. She stood, frozen. Unarmed. Unsure how she could help.

"Oh, look... the subject of our latest sweet dreamsssss," the demon crooned, tilting its head so it could look past Kass and fix her with those black, bulbous eyes.

She could discern no depth or emotion there, and a chill fingered down her spine. She straightened, calling her own magic forward to lurk beneath her skin. A comfort, if nothing more.

"Begone, Ozul! This is my last day." Kass's voice broke. "May I not have peace?"

The demon cackled. "Oh, no. You receive no peace for what you will do to her come nightfall."

"Be silent, you wretch!" He cursed it.

Venya frowned. "What does it mean?"

"Nothing." He sliced a hand through the air, but he did not turn to her, still holding that dagger towards the demon.

"Liar," crooned the demon.

Venya did not miss the way Kass's shoulders stiffened.

The demon continued, "Maiden, you are doomed to die, and his will be the hand that enacts it."

"W-what? I don't understand."

"See for yourself," the demon said with a vicious smile. It surged forward, bowling Kass over. He fell aside, caught off guard.

And then, that demon was upon Venya, and she did not even have a second to feel terror as it gripped her face in its brutally clawed, long-fingered hands, and pressed its face, teeth bared, against hers. It breathed darkness into her mouth. Her eyes rolled back as the world fell away.

"No!" was the last thing she heard, a frantic cry from Kass. Her whole body was paralysed, and she felt nothing, save for the burning touch of that demon upon her cheeks.

A vision unfurled in the darkness. A stone cave. Lit by fire. The light threw jagged shadows around the space. It was so *cold*, but a fire burned in her blood, and she struggled. Why did she struggle? The sluggish thought took a moment to answer.

Large hands gripped her. Familiar ones. An arm around her waist, trapping one arm at her side. Another hand, an iron grip around her free wrist, forcing it down. Her legs kicked nought but air. She twisted, rearing her head back so she could see who carried her.

Her heart dropped.

Kass.

He looked *savage*. A stranger as he glared down at her with cold, dark eyes, no hint of that molten gold and amber sparkle that had enchanted her.

"Kass, no!" she heard herself scream, but the voice was disembodied. Whatever vision the demon had plunged her into not marrying with the free thought she still had.

He carried her further, and when she twisted and slipped in his grasp, he dragged her. Her feet scuffed the floor, her boots catching on lumps. Overhead, the cave roof soared away, stalactites poised like daggers to fall above their heads.

"Uhn!" The breath was knocked out of her and pain slammed through her back as he lifted and crashed her onto a large, flat slab.

She glanced around. It was the very centre of a huge cavern, lit by faelights that hovered, red and angry above them both.

"What are you doing?" She struggled, but Kass pinned her down with the weight of his body. Fear lashed through her. The encounter was not intimate. This time, he did not lay between her legs. This time, he forced her hands into shackles, and bound her ankles to the slab with something she could not see, for he had restrained her so tightly, she could hardly lift her head and shoulders.

His eyes weren't his own, she realised with a jolt. They were the precise, bottomless black of the demon's eyes. She struggled against her bonds.

"Kass? Are you in there? Kass! Let me out. What are you doing?!"

She had a dreadful feeling that she knew. He turned back to her—and her worst fears were confirmed. He—*it*—brandished that dark knife. Was that Kass, or was that the demon?

"Feeding," he crooned. "I can feed the demon your life instead of mine. Yours will be forfeit, but I shall survive."

No...

As he raised the blade and smiled viciously at her, his

expression so filled with callous glee that she did not recognise him, there was no time to doubt every moment they had ever had together.

She felt the blade punch deep a second after betrayal stabbed her heart, cutting the breath from her. And she watched as he revelled in her death and the world went black.

VENYA SHUDDERED. The demon dropped her, and she fell onto the floor hard, reeling as the vision faded. Her body stung from the impact on the hard floor.

"No!" Kass roared from somewhere above her. There was movement. Light and dark flashing, shadows and faelight dancing around the room as they moved. Crashing. Shouting.

And then, silence.

"Venya!" Kass panted with the exertion of it, his hot breath rolling over her. He grasped her arm, and she wrenched away with a ghostly memory of the pain from the demon's vision. He held her in precisely the same place just above the wrist.

"Are you alright? What happened?"

She staggered to her feet and backed away from him, crashing into the hearth. The demon was gone. Pata lurked, battered and injured, leaking magic, on the far side of the room.

"You! You… you *cur!*" The curse felt like filth upon her tongue, but it did not come close to how sullied that vision had made her feel. "You were planning to betray me? All along?" Her voice cracked.

His face dropped and paled. "Wait. The demon. What did he show you?" Kass shot to his feet.

"He showed me enough," Venya sobbed angrily. "You coward!"

He flinched at the word.

"You only kept me here so you could sacrifice me in your stead. *How could you?*" The pain of his betrayal laced those words, and he fell back as though she had hit him.

"Venya, I promise you, I would not—"

"Tell me that it is not true." She faced him, her entire body shaking, her fists clenched.

Kass's mouth hung open, but no words came out. She felt the depth of his emotion as he stared at her, aghast, but she knew he could not tell her otherwise, because to do so would be a lie. And the fae could not lie.

"You…" She shook her head. Words failed her.

"It's not like that. I promise," he said desperately, stepping forward and trying to catch her hands in his, but she sidestepped him and twisted away, keeping her distance. "At the start… things were different. I was desperate! But as I… As you… I could not. Believe me. *Please.* I could not hurt you."

Her chest felt as though it had caved in. Too much pain. Too much shock.

"I trusted you."

He had no reply. What could he say?

She pushed past him and ran out before he saw her hot angry tears spill.

He did not follow her.

CHAPTER FORTY-TWO

Kass leaned heavily against the hearth, resting his head against the cool stone. That cursed demon writhed inside him. He felt Ozul's glee as if it were his own, but it only made him feel nauseous, overlaid on his own overwhelming guilt.

He could not defend himself against her. He could not lie. The demon had shown her the truth of his own nightmares, it seemed. The truth of what he had intended to do to her—though only at first, and before he had ever truly thought through the despicable depths of the crime he would have to commit to save his own soul.

He did not deserve one shred of her. What he had intended to do, however seriously or not, was indefensible. She would depart on Starfall eve, and he had no damned right to stop her.

"Are you happy now?" he screamed at the demon inside him. "You shall have me, and you lost her."

"*I did not lose her,*" countered the demon, uncurling lazily within him. "*I shall have you and then I shall enjoy hunting her down and ending her too. It shall still come to pass, though in a different manner and place. I believe I shall wear your face to add to her fear and despair."*

Kass crumpled to the floor as sobs of despair shook him. It had all been for nothing. It was all hopeless. Instead of succumbing to the weakness of his desire for her, allowing them both to be distracted for precious hours, he should have made sure she had left whilst there was still a chance of her outrunning this accursed demon.

Now, they were both doomed to die. And worst of all, she would die believing that he had betrayed her.

After all, he had.

CHAPTER FORTY-THREE

Venya took the stairs two at a time to her tower. She had precious little, but it would have to do. She had to leave at once, before Kass found her, caught her, and dragged her to that cave. Fear coursed through her alongside roaring anger and a river of pain at his betrayal and her own foolishness.

Her fingers stumbled over the clasp of her cloak as she donned it. Venya forced herself to take a deep, shuddering breath. To make a mistake now would be life and death. She was to venture into the Wildewood in the middle of a winter's night with no horse, no provisions, and no hope—but she had no other choice. She could not remain here with him, knowing that he would betray her that very day to save his own cursed skin. A sob burst forth.

She had her pack. One strap was torn where it had ripped free of Boy's saddle. She shouldered it nonetheless. She would stop by the kitchen for any food she could grab on the way out. Days from hospitable lands, and in the grip of the first winter snows, she could not count on finding anything palatable on the way.

Lastly, she grabbed her dagger and strapped it to her hip. It hung there, familiar as her own limbs, but a strange weight after being absent since her arrival. It felt insubstantial against what she would face out in the Wildewood and, she was willing to admit, against *him*. She would not let him take her willingly to her own death. She would fight tooth and nail with whatever resources she had at her disposal, even if it was hopeless.

Venya scurried down the stairs and sprinted down the halls, heading for the library. She was not sure if it was spite, anger, hurt, or some combination that drove her there. Into the darkened room she burst, swiping her chain from the desk there. He would not have it. He did not deserve it. Whether he saved himself or not was nothing to do with her. She would not be used and taken for a fool. She shoved the links in her pack, the magic tingling through her skin as she buried them at the bottom. Insubstantial as they were, they weighed little. It would be no penance to carry them too.

From the library, she took one wrong turn on her way to the kitchen. Into her pack went a loaf of bread, a pot of butter—she would scoop the damned stuff out with her fingers if she had to—several cuts of ham, and a lump of cheese. She drew the pouch shut and slung the good strap over her head so it sat across her body on one shoulder like a satchel. A little ungainly, but better than nothing. Her water-skin, though empty, was in the bottom too. She could pack that with snow and drink it when it had melted.

A scrape behind her made her jump out of her skin.

Pata watched her.

"Don't fight me," she warned the construct. "I do not want to hurt you, but I will defend myself." She had no idea what her odds were against the construct.

"Please do not leave," Pata begged as she pushed past him.

She scoffed.

"He needs you."

She whirled on the construct, her temper rising. "How *dare* you? I owe him nothing. Not after this. Leave me alone."

"You cannot go out there. Not by yourself; not in the dark. It is folly. You will be dead before dawn."

Venya growled, "Watch me. I'd like to see anything try and stop me right now." She would eviscerate anything that stepped in her way, with the mood she was in.

"Venya…"

She left Pata behind and did not turn to see if he followed. Shadows yawned as she strode to the front door, and no one came to stop her. Her fraught senses reached out into the night, desperate for the first sign of a threat, but nothing and no one came for her. Not him. There was a hole where her heart was. It *hurt* and the ragged edges seethed with an ire that burned her.

She stepped from the front door into a wall of bitter cold that had her shrugging her cloak tighter and lifting the hood. This would be a painful journey, but her survival depended upon it. There was only one thing that threatened to keep her, and even that wavered.

She had been waiting for the construct to return with news of her mother. But the realisation dawned on her. *It was probably all a lie. A huge joke at my expense.*

The construct had been fake, she was certain. Why would he help her genuinely? No. He had tricked her. She had been too blind to see it. And now, she had put herself in grave danger—and, she realised with a further cracking of her heart—doomed her mother.

Whilst she had been in blissful ignorance, assuming all was well in hand, her mother would have been suffering, breathing her last. Shame swiftly turned Venya's thoughts away from that glorious day and night in the cabin where she had given into the pure selfishness of her own pleasure.

Maybe her mother was already dead. Venya crumpled. *No.* She could not think like that.

Whilst she still drew breath, there was hope. There was a chance. The construct may have been false, the cure nothing but a lie, some silly liquid in a vial that was less effective than a nettle tea, but she was alive and heading home.

Mother will be dead by the time you return. Today is Starfall. She probably already is. That was the longest they gave her.

Venya had thought that her mother would be cured and whole by now. Never realising the depths of Kass's betrayal. All the while… *If I had turned around immediately, maybe I could have made it home in time to see her. Say goodbye.*

She knew that would have been an impossible stretch. It would have taken many weeks to return home, especially without a mount. Either way, she had seen her mother for the very last time.

Tears flowed freely, freezing on her cheeks as Venya trudged out of the courtyard and onto the track outside. She had no map, nothing but the stars to guide her. Leander and Arielle hung to the south, taunting. She turned away. North. And looked for the guiding star that would see her home to Pelenor. It would be weeks by the time she returned on foot.

She'll be gone. She is *gone. It's my fault. And I couldn't stop it.*

CHAPTER FORTY-FOUR

Kass exploded in rage and self-loathing, destroying his newly repaired room and blazing down the hallway in a streak of carnage, unable to take his anger out on himself and venting it on the building instead.

It was hopeless.

He was going to die, knowing he had failed, in the end, to protect her. The one who had become, so unexpectedly, the most important thing to him, only he had been too damned stupid and blind and scared to see it. He would die knowing she hated him.

That was the most painful realisation of all. Self-pity and self-loathing swirled inside him as he painted a raw and brutal canvas upon the blasted halls of his castle to reflect the shattered mess inside.

Soon, the demon would be free and worse would come to pass.

Venya would die at Ozul's hands if she yet remained alive, knowing he had betrayed her. Would any shred of his consciousness remain? Would he watch her through the demon's eyes as it ended her slowly and painfully?

Kass closed his eyes and punched the wall. It reverberated with the force of his anger, and when he looked, the very stone had crumpled and cracked. His fist throbbed. Angry and seething, his magic healed it in moments.

"Are you quite done yet?" Pata's voice was as ice-cold as the rising storm outside.

It was light. When had it gotten light? Had his rampage lasted all night?

Kass glared at Pata, baring his teeth at the big cat. But Pata only snarled back. "Whilst you're in here breaking things like a fool and feeling sorry for yourself, she is out there in that freezing-cold storm."

Something in Kass lurched—concern. He crushed it.

"Would you see her die of cold?"

"She will die either way," Kass said bitterly. "The cold is probably a kinder death."

Pata stalked forward, lashing his tail. "I never thought you capable of such despicable cowardice, Kassimir de Rochefort. You are *detestable* and you ought to be ashamed. When did you lose your honour?"

Anger flared, and Kass hurled a bolt of fire at the construct.

Pata leapt aside, yowling, and charged him, knocking Kass into the wall.

They circled each other, both hissing. "I am not your enemy," Pata snarled. "He is deep inside you."

Before Kass could answer, a shadow crossed the window between them, and something heavy thudded onto the sill. Kass blinked. A sharp tap on the glass came from the other side.

Automatically, Kass surged forward to open the window,

and a giant bird flopped in, feathers sticking out at all angles, and snow clinging to its claws.

The eagle construct.

Kass's stomach clenched. He stuck out his arm, and the eagle hopped on. This close, he saw the magic fraying on the edge of its feathers. Its tail glittered, littering golden sparks onto the floor. He pushed magic into it to shore up the enchantment.

"Show me," he breathed to it, and locked eyes with it.

Those green eyes widened, and a stream of golden magic coursed between the two of them. The journey the eagle had taken relayed to him in super-speed. He traced its path as it flew over forests, mountains, seas, plains, and cities until it eventually circled to land in a verdant valley where the most exquisite palace lay, an isolated jewel amongst the wilds of that country.

He saw Venya's mother—instantly recognisable. Her daughter was her spitting image, though far younger and but for her violet eyes, which Kass now guessed she had taken from her father. The violet-eyed elf who examined the construct. Kass heard his grave voice through a distance, muted and muffled. The eagle's magic was nearly spent. He examined the construct with suspicion, but tears were shed when Venya's letter was discovered, and then the vial.

This female, Venya's mother, was so pale and wasted. Kass watched as, after a flurry of movement—elves coming and going, many peering at the construct with open curiosity or suspicion, as it waited to see its duty fulfilled—the medicine was administered. Kass could barely breathe. The construct remained for three days to see it begin to take effect—as his own small letter had instructed—before they sent it back with…

A small letter dangled from the eagle's raised leg. It

offered it to him. Kass untied it with shaking hands and scanned the spiky handwriting inside.

The medicine had worked. Her condition was already miraculously improving. The healers expected her to make an unprecedented recovery, as Venya would see for herself upon her return. Thanks, too. *Extend her our love and gratitude, and you yourself, dear sir, for your assistance rendered. We hope to see you both soon to tell you in person.*

It was signed, most sincerely, by her father. *Dimitrius Vaeri Mortris of House Ellarian.*

His hand shook so much that the letter fell from his grasp. "It worked. The cure worked." His voice sounded hollow.

"And Venya will never know." Pata spat the words angrily. "Who even knows where she is, if she is still alive in this damned wood."

That knocked the breath from him. "O-of course she is alive," he spluttered, because he could not face the alternative.

Pata snarled in his face. "Do the right thing, you coward. Instead of taking out your anger and self-pity on your abode, instead of cutting off your nose to spite your face, *do the right thing.*"

Kass moaned and dropped his head into a hand. "It is too late." *You damned fool. What have you done?* Pata was quite correct. She was out there all alone, and she had been gone overnight. The most dangerous time to traverse the Wildewood. A surge of urgency had him sweeping his tangle of hair back before Pata's retort.

"It is *never* too late." Pata was right.

"I have failed her already, unforgivably so. I cannot fail her again. If she yet lives, if she has somehow managed to survive this damn forest, I must find her. She needs to know."

His attention fell to the bird. "You cannot finish your task yet, friend. You must show this to her. She must know her mother survived and will be well." *If nothing else, perhaps that will go some way towards redeeming me.* That was such a foolish hope, he dismissed it immediately.

He ran a feather-light hand across the bird's head, imbuing it with more strength, shoring up its failing magic. It would endure maybe another day. He had to find her first.

Perhaps dying would not be so bad if he was able to see her one last time—and give her the news she had so craved from home.

CHAPTER FORTY-FIVE

Venya walked until dawn and did not falter until darkness came again the next night—Starfall night—when she was bone-achingly tired and so cold she could not feel her feet anymore.

The Wildewood had been eerily quiet and lonely, covered in a shroud of snow. She had used her magic to quieten the sound of her passage and deaden her scent, travelling ever north. She had not taken the road, but forged a more direct path through the forest. She did not want to pass those barrows again.

Her magic tugged her onwards to a treeless hollow. Venya followed it, half suspicious. She felt power ahead and did not know what that meant. Through the bare-branched trees she crunched, her cloak sweeping away some of her tracks, shushing over the crystalline surface behind her. Her vantage point crested the horizon and she halted.

Ahead, a wide, shallow bowl lay in the landscape. It was entirely bare of trees. Not a branch crossed the threshold of that summit line, although the tangle crowded close to it as though an invisible line cut them off. In the centre, a stone circle of a dozen stones stood. Different sizes, shapes, and heights, pointing like jagged teeth up into the sky. Between them lay protection and beneath them… magic.

Venya sped down the hill. As she passed into the circle, the featherlight touch of old magic brushed through her. She slipped off her gloves and dug through the snow to the flattened moss and grass below. She plunged her hands into it, the frigid wetness slicking to her palms, her fingers tangling in that green carpet. Down she sent her awareness, into the power beating far below. A wellspring. Much like a water spring, only filled with magic, where the barriers between the magic source deep under the surface weakened, crept up through fissures, and leached power to the surface.

It was heady as she drank in that power, replenishing her tired, aching bones, wiping away the cares of the road, and filling her with hope. She had found a safe spot for the night, she hoped. Venya cast her eye around the stones. Snow dusted them, pooled around them, and crusted the moss and lichen that clung to those old stones. She paced around the circle, placing a palm on each stone in turn. They were cold, yes, but each one tingled as she touched it, as though they greeted her too.

"I will stay the night and move on come the morning," she told the place quietly. Her eyes glanced across the horizon. She could not see beyond the dip. It would have made her feel vulnerable without that well of power there. As it was, it made her feel safe, nestled amongst those stones, away from predatory eyes. "Please protect me?"

The stones did not answer. A lonely wind blew, whistling through the trees and rustling the forest around her. Despite the white blanket helping illuminate the space, night had fallen. She did not risk a fire. Just in case.

Venya donned her gloves and dug out a nook before one

of the stones. She planted her back against it, crouching with her cloak wrapped around her. It would be a long and uncomfortable night. She doubted she would sleep, but at least with that bank of power below her, she had all the strength to draw on to ensure she would be warm without a fire. She ate a ration of the food she had taken before settling to silence for the night, left only with her thoughts as a companion.

They were not kind.

You have been such a fool, Ven. She sighed. *You trusted another with your most important burden—and he let you down. Distracted you.* Her jaw clenched—both at her own foolishness and his hatefulness. She had shared every part of herself, body and soul with him and all along he had intended to kill her.

Her throat closed. She could not bear to think about it. Too painful. Never again. It was a lesson learned. A hard one.

She hated that he had brought her closer to peace and happiness than she had ever known—and taken it away so cruelly, too. But the fact remained. If nothing else, was he right in that, at least? Did she really need to carry the guilt she had struggled with all those years?

She hated to admit it, but Kass was right. She had not chosen to be born. Her mother had accepted the risks of having a child—and some of those risks had not worked out in her favour. That was not Venya's fault. She had carried a burden never meant for her.

What a waste of energy for all those years. It had gotten her nowhere in the end. No closer to her own peace or happiness. No closer to helping her mother—whether for guilt or love.

A branch snapped nearby.

Venya's head snapped up. It was dark, but the snow

reflected the moonlight plentifully. Shadows moved down the sides of the depression towards the stone circle. One, two, three to the north and east. Another four from the south.

Her senses fired up, nerves coursing through her. Venya reached out with her magic. Beast? Friend or foe?

Worse.

Darkyn.

She could not hold out against so many. Not on her own, practically unarmed save for a small dagger and magic shored up by the wellspring's power. Not in the realm of night, when the Darkyn were strongest.

There was no time to plan. No time to think. They were almost at the edge of the stone circle. Venya sprang to her feet, sucked all the magic she could channel from that wellspring towards her, and unleashed a giant blast of light.

CHAPTER FORTY-SIX

Kassimir passed through shadow and night, following Venya's faint trail through the starlit forest. For miles and miles he tracked her—how had she gotten this far on foot? His heart swelled with pride and relief. So far, she was alive. He had found no evidence of her demise, no trace of trouble. She had done well at concealing her passage sufficiently that even he had trouble tracking her at times.

Urgency drove him, every heartbeat hammering the passing of another second they were parted, another second she could come to harm. The eagle soared high above, following his trail, tethered to him by the bonds of his magic.

The moon high above illuminated the way, dappling light through the forest onto the snow-laden ground. Her tracks slowed as they approached a rise, but fresh tracks had joined the way and with a stab of fear, Kass realised what they belonged to—Darkyn—and that she was vastly outnumbered. He sped over the hill just as light bloomed ahead.

He threw up an arm to shield his eyes until the flare died, then he surged forward.

The stone circle. The wellspring. He came here to replenish, sometimes. It was usually a safe haven in the forest. Creatures were drawn to its power, certainly, but inside the stone circle, nothing could pass. The Darkyn were immune from that.

Half a dozen of them slipped between the standing stones, advancing upon the lone figure in the centre of the ring.

Venya.

No!

He roared his challenge, hurtling down the slope towards them, magic brimming inside him before it erupted.

CHAPTER FORTY-SEVEN

At the roar, Venya's terror multiplied tenfold, before she recognised that blurred mass.

Kass.

For a moment, she could not believe he had come—and a moment was all they had. She possessed no time besides to consider the ramifications of what that meant before the demons, who had fallen back at her blast of light, advanced once more, oozing noxious night. Dizzy on the fumes of it soaking into each breath, Venya swayed. She pulled on that magic deep beneath her feet and kept them at bay with whiplashes of light that had them screaming so loud her ears rang.

And then Kass was amongst their mass. He moved like the wind, taking them out one by one with magic and his dark blade. Back-to-back with him, Venya fought her corner, forcing those demons back with shields of light until they fled into the dark.

Kass gave chase. Their dying shrieks reached her moments later. He returned at a sprint, skidding to a halt at her side and spinning in a slow circle. His wide eyes reflected moonlight and snow—their gold and silver lit up—no hint of the demon's dark possession.

There was no hint of a demon left, either. All dead or fled.

The tension and fear left Venya, her shoulders loosening, but as Kass turned to her, up went the walls again. She backed away, her dagger held high.

He made to sweep towards her, his arms outstretched—but the relief and emotion turned to shock as he saw her dagger. He halted.

"Venya. It's me. I mean you no harm."

She shook her head and gritted her teeth. Her whole body trembled with shock and exertion. She felt dead on her feet, but she would not give in to him.

"Stay away."

Emotions bled through her. Without him, she might already be dead. She was relieved for his help and, on a deeper level, relieved to see him. She still cared, damn it, and she hated herself for it. It was a weakness only she could fix, and she needed time to cut him from where he had lodged inside her heart.

His face fell. Hurt flashed through him. She did not care. How could she? He planned to kill her to save his own worthless hide. What did his hurt feelings matter?

"You need to see this, at least," he said, "and then I will trouble you no further, aside from seeing you safely from these woods and on your way."

A blur had her blood rushing and the dagger raised again, until she saw it was the eagle construct, landing in a flurry before her.

"What is this?"

"Proof of my good intentions. For what little they are worth." He spoke through a clenched jaw and his eyes burned into her, but she refused to meet his gaze. "It returns from your homeland with news. *Good* news, Venya. Watch."

She froze as the eagle turned to her. It flared its wings wide and met her stare. Magic streamed between them, and a vision settled, warm and golden, in her mind. *Home.* Her family. He could not have forged that, down to the smallest details she had never shown him. A lump grew in her throat as she watched it. And when it was done, the eagle—its feathers now tattered and ragged, disintegrating into gold— turned to Kass.

He placed a hand on its head. "Thank you, friend."

In a swirl of warmth and magic, the creature disintegrated before her. Its feathers scattered and its body fell into a golden web that disappeared into nothing, leaving nothing but tiny trailing embers of light that sunk into the snow and vanished.

"Is that the truth?" Her voice broke.

"I swear it," he replied solemnly.

Venya choked on a sob but could not stop it. Relief broke down every barrier in her and tears streamed freely. She cried into her hands, not wanting him to bear witness to any of this. Her mother was safe. Alive. Well. *Healing.*

It was more than she had dared hope for. More than she could have ever asked for. She had believed the worst. But he had sworn what the eagle had shown to be the truth. That meant he had not betrayed her in this too. For herself—for what she had thought they had—she mourned and raged, but for her mother, she was so relieved she could hardly bear the strength of feeling rushing through her.

She's alive. Thank the heavens.

CHAPTER FORTY-EIGHT

He watched her crumble and forced himself not to go to her. She despised him. Rightly so. It was not his place to comfort her. Pain erupted in his chest nonetheless. It had felt so good to see her again, the sheer relief of realising she was alive, though in grave danger. To stand shoulder to shoulder with her, working together as one unit to overcome those Darkyn, had been an honour.

It cut him that it would probably be the last time. She would leave and he would see her safely away before returning to his homelands. He had to see her far away by midnight. Before his curse broke and the demon within was unleashed and devoured him.

He had one burning task to do before it did.

As her sobs subsided and she dragged her tears away on her sleeves, he sank to his knees in the churned-up snow before her.

"Venya. I am so sorry. I failed you, so many times." He forced himself to look up at her.

She watched him, clenching her shaking fists at her side, her jaw stiff.

He swallowed. "I will admit when you came, it was as though Arielle herself had fallen from the heavens. You were a gift. I have been so..." He licked his lips. These were hard words to get out. He had never said them to himself, let alone anyone else. "...so scared and alone for so long. My hope had faded to nothing. I did not want to die. That was my prime motivation, and I will admit that. I am flawed and weak, and I am scared to face the demon. I know but a fraction of the unending torture he will exact upon me as revenge.

"It was easy to consider placing a faceless stranger in my stead. Saving myself at their expense. You are so much nobler than I am. I am sure you would meet your fate with far more grace, but I am not so good-hearted. Yet, when I looked upon your face, I knew I could not. I could *never.*" His shoulders slumped.

"Why else do you think I offered our arrangement? I wanted so desperately to find another way. Even if it were foolish to hope that a union between us would help me outrun my fate, or that the extra time would find me a solution after so long. As I grew to know you, I felt as I have never felt before. I have never cared for another as much as I care for you. That time in the cabin... every moment of it was *real.* I would have stayed there with you forever, had I been able to. You enchant me. You fascinate me. You give me hope. Hope that there is a way out of my own inexorable doom."

He dragged a hand through his hair and swallowed. "I thought with your idea, perhaps there would be. Now, my doom approaches and all is lost—for me, at least. I would see you safely away and far from here ere that happens. I will gladly go to my death, knowing you are safe. Please, accept my deepest apologies. I never should have kept this from you. I did not wish you to find out. To have you know the depths of my cowardice. To know you would think so little of me for all I have done. I demand nothing of you, but I beg for your forgiveness."

At her feet, he bowed his head. She would never forgive him, he was quite sure, but he had to ask. If she did… perhaps he could go to his death a little lighter and a little braver for her favour.

CHAPTER FORTY-NINE

Venya had not known how deeply she needed to hear her mother was safe and would be well—and his apology. It hit something in her core to see how sorry he was, to know that he must have tracked her relentlessly and unwaveringly to ensure she was safe and to ensure that she knew the truth. That he truly cared. That he had not taken her for a fool with false promises of her mother's health to lure her in, to seduce her for his own fun, to betray her without a shred of decency or guilt. His actions showed so much more than any words could.

"Say something. Anything," he pleaded, looking up at her.

"I don't know what to say," Venya said with a groan, dropping to her knees before him. The snow melted beneath her, seeping through her leggings, wet and cold. She shook her head. "I'm so confused. I do not know what is real, and what is not. I thought you had lied about *everything*, all to lure me in. That the cure for my mother was simply another ruse to make me stay, remain biddable. I thought she was *dead*." Her voice cracked.

"No," he said fiercely, and snatched her hands up, pressing reassurance into them.

Her tears flowed freely, fear and hurt and anger leaking out. "I thought you had used me for pleasure. That you cast me aside when you realised you no longer needed the ruse of an arranged marriage to keep me, because you had realised I was so foolishly infatuated with you, I would stay of my own accord."

His reply was hoarse. "That's not how it is. Skies, I am such a damned idiot. I am so sorry for causing you such pain, Venya. Every ounce of what we shared was *real*. Is real, if you still wanted me."

"I wanted the peace and happiness," she said sadly. "I have never found such solace, and I craved more. I wanted you."

"WANTED?" he dared to question, holding his breath. *Past tense.* His stomach clenched. This glorious female before him… and he had been stupid enough to let her slip through his fingers, to push her away, to betray her for his own fears.

She paused, eyes darting to meet his, falling to the ground, and then slowly rising once more. He still held her hands as he knelt across from her in the snow. She had not pulled away. It tugged on something inside his chest, that he had not been utterly forsaken yet, much as he deserved it.

"Want," she admitted in a whisper. "Still want."

Something unlocked inside him and he took a gulp of life-giving air, tasting hope upon it.

"I want this for myself." Her voice wavered, but grew stronger. "I have lived my whole life in service of others, carrying a guilt I am only now realising was never truly mine to bear. I want to choose for myself now, and…" She swallowed, licked her lips. "I might be a fool, but my heart pulls me towards *you*."

It was all he wanted. And everything he could not accept.

"You cannot," he said hollowly. "Not now—it is too late."

She bared her teeth at him. "You came for me. No matter the danger to you."

"Of course I did. It took me long enough to come to my senses, but I could not leave you alone to your fate."

"And I cannot leave you to yours." Her eyes gleamed in the darkness, violet in the faint moonlight.

"There's not enough ti—"

"There is time enough to try," she said, the set of her jaw brooking no argument.

"I am doomed," he said on a breath. "Please, do not doom yourself with me." There was no way. He did not dare to hope anymore. That demon was a visceral weight, dragging his soul down into the darkness. He barely had any time left. "Let me make sure you are gone. Safe. I will meet my fate with the courage I should have had all along."

But she only shook her head and turned upon him a question he had asked her in good faith. "Do you trust me?"

CHAPTER FIFTY

Venya would not give up hope. She was resilience personified. She stood, tugging Kass with her, and staring at him, trying to imbue him with the same determination she felt lining her.

"You told me that like calls to like, and opposites repel. We will set a trap. Your demon will emerge, but in the time, place, and manner of our choosing."

She still had the chain. They could do this. She was sure of it. She opened her mouth to speak, but he cut her off.

"I do not have the grimoire. I have nothing. We have nothing." He groaned and covered his face with his hands.

She pulled them away. "I have a plan. I promise."

"Don't tell me it," he said desperately, pulling away from her grasp and taking a step back. He jabbed a finger at his temple. "He's in here. He knows my innermost thoughts. I cannot deceive him. He sees all. He knows all."

Fear curled through her. He was right. In him lived the evil they had to defeat. He had to be blind to the plan—until the very last second, that was. Venya swallowed, took a steadying breath, and stepped forward, sliding her hands up his chest. "I understand. Trust me. I will see that we do this, together."

"How can we, when whatever I know will betray us?"

She had never heard him sound so doubtful. For a moment, it made her wonder too, but she steeled herself. She had to be strong enough for both of them, for just a little longer. Did she believe in herself?

Yes.

That gave her a tingle of nerves and the confidence to rise to her tiptoes and press her forehead to his. "At the right moment, and you will know precisely when that is, sever the bond. I will do the rest."

"How…?"

"You will know," she promised. She repeated, "At the right moment. Sever the connection. Can you do that?"

His breath fluttered raggedly in the night air, pluming between them. He nodded.

"Venya," he murmured.

She stiffened, willing away the flip in her stomach. "Yes?"

"May I kiss you? One last time?"

Venya pressed her eyes shut. She wanted it and did not. But fire ran through her, on that edge of aliveness that emboldened her. What were they doing, if not daring to defy the odds? If they died, what would be the harm? If they lived… this could be just the start.

"Yes," she breathed.

A small sound escaped him and then his hands were on her cheeks, pulling her closer. His lips bruised hers with the sweet intensity of his kiss as they both pressed all those unsaid things into that one small gesture. They pulled apart a moment later—too soon—for there was no more time. The zenith of Starfall had arrived.

Chills crawled up Venya's back as they both tipped their

heads to the sky to watch the first streak, then the second, then a hundred more as the annual shower of stars erupted, racing across the heavens in a shimmering veil.

Starfall.

Venya soaked in that beautiful sight of shattered crystals falling across the sky—and then Kass grunted at her side and doubled over.

To see her watch that meteor shower with awe momentarily distracted Kass from the impending doom upon them both. The moon and starlight above, reflecting off the snow below, illuminated her with an almost otherworldly glow. In that moment, she did indeed look as wondrous to him as Arielle must have looked to Leander, and in that moment, he felt as unworthy as a mortal to look upon her.

He felt the curse break like a ricochet through him. Kass grunted and hunched over as it stole his breath. Half in the frosty night with Venya beside him, half inside himself, he felt the awful snap of the curse's demise. The night breeze was drowned out by that internal shriek of pure euphoria as the demon punched through its restraints, and like glass upon stone, they shattered into nothing.

"Kass?" Her voice came from a distance.

He pushed her away as gently as he could and stumbled back into the centre of the stone circle.

"Stay back," he grunted, shaking with the exertion. The demon already fought him for power over his body, his voice, his mind. It waxed as he waned. He could not hold on much longer. He gasped in a shred of breath, winded by the ferocious power of the denizen.

He had underestimated Ozul.

Panic shuddered through him, and bought him a few moments as it shoved the demon down. If this went wrong, they were both dead, and for the first time, he felt more fear for her, for someone else, than he did for himself. He could not bear it. He could not let her down. He would not see her die for his mistakes.

"I choose you," he howled as invisible claws raked furrows down his back, plucking on every nerve, twisting and stabbing for maximum pain. "I will always choose you, Venya. No matter what I might say or do now... that is not me. Remember that. Please." His voice cracked on the last word and a howl erupted. He could do nothing but surrender to the demon breaking him from the inside out, and hope that they would both live to see the other side of this.

CHAPTER FIFTY-ONE

*V*enya saw the moment that Kass's eyes changed, from sparkling silver reflecting the snow crystals below and stars above, plunging to the deepest depths of black. A moment later, a cruel smile unfurled upon his face, making him entirely unrecognisable. He straightened, curling and uncurling his fingers, flexing his arms, and rolling his shoulders, as though that demon were testing the control it had of this new flesh and blood it possessed.

"You cannot hope to prevail, elf," it taunted her through his mouth, with his voice, stretching its neck side to side, at leisure. Confidence oozed from it.

Venya backed away to stand between two of those giant stone sentinels and pulled the magic up from the earth below. "I see you, Kass. I know you're in there still." Her nerves, that flying fear, calmed in the face of talking to him. A distraction. A necessary one to make her forget the danger she was now in.

"Yes, he is," the demon agreed. "He can see and hear and feel it all. He will experience everything I do to you, elf. I will end you and he will feel it to the fullest and know he is help-less. I shall enjoy reaping his pain."

"We can do this, Kass," Venya said as calmly as she could, drawing that magic up. It formed golden threads that wove between the stones into an elegant web. It arced up further and further, encasing the space in a dome that extended both above and below the ground. With the magic of the well-spring exceeding her powers beyond anything she could have accomplished alone, it was almost effortless. She would need to save her energy for the hardest part of this.

The demon hissed at the brightness of that magic. "Stop that."

Venya laughed in defiance and pulled the net tighter. It wove between the very stones now. She needed Kass to wrest back control at the opportune moment. No sooner. No later.

"Leave him now," she said, levelling a stare at the thing inside Kass, focusing her attention on those black eyes, and not how unnatural and unnerving it was to look upon his face and see a stranger.

"I do not cede. You will have to kill your lover to see me ended."

"Liar." She knew enough of demons from her extensive lifetime of research to know that killing the host only freed the denizen to find a new one if it desired. In this case, she had no doubt it would be her.

"Kass. It's nearly time. I know you can hear me." Venya settled her stance wider. Her whole body tensed. How would this play out? She had no idea. Terror laced every breath.

"We're going to do this," she shouted into the night, to herself as well as him. "This ends. Your guilt. Mine. Every-thing we've carried for all these years. All of it. It ends *now*."

It was all going to burn and they would rise like phoenixes from the ashes. There was no room for fear.

"I have waited five hundred years for this moment, and I will waste no more time," Kass—the demon within him—snarled, and rushed her. She tried to twist aside, but he was too agile. He wrenched her back, gripped her by the neck, lifted her off her feet with inhuman strength, and slammed her back into one of the standing stones.

Pain jolted through her. Winded, she choked with that hand around her neck. His face pressed close, those black eyes all she could see. This was too like the wight attack—except his hold burned. Too hopeless. He was too strong. She pulled on the magic tight, but already, her head swam and she could not catch any breath around the tight grip of his hand on her neck.

Fear paralysed her, but only for a second before desperation kicked in. She scrabbled at the hand holding her throat, scratching at Kass's flesh, so desperate to ensure her own survival she could not feel a shred of guilt for slicing her nails across the back of his hand. But it did not work.

Before her, Kass's face, frozen in an inhuman snarl, faded in and out of her failing vision. Those black eyes oozed potent malice—with none of the spark that had attracted her to the fae—and promised her nothing but death. The demon would not relinquish his hold, and Venya's strength faded.

CHAPTER FIFTY-TWO

Kassimir had turned inwards, trying to wrest control of his body back from the demon, when her cry of pain, swiftly cut off, pulled his attention to the surface. He watched through his own eyes, sensed through his own body, as he slammed her against that sentinel of stone.

He *felt* the vibration of her cry cut off against the skin of his palm. It unleashed him. With a rush of strength born of desperation, he tugged on the wellspring below the stone circle, that vast, endless whorl of power. Kass reared up, surging through himself, scouring that demon's poisonous control from every muscle, every vein, every artery.

THE HAND RELEASED, and Venya collapsed to the ground in a heap, crunching into the snow beneath her. She gulped a desperate breath—tensing when Kass's hands wrenched her wrists up, pulling her to her feet.

"Are you hurt?" His eyes were wild and desperate—and silver-gold.

Her chest expanded with a fresh breath. She could not reply, so desperately sucking air into her dazed body. Her throat still felt constricted, like a rope was tied around it and pulled tight.

"The knife," she croaked. "Now. Ready it."

KASS UNSHEATHED THE SHADOW BLADE. His heart lurched. If this went wrong, he would die. This was the moment he had feared all along—the one he had spent centuries running from. Underneath his skin, that demon railed against his iron will, now in firm control of his body. It cracked through the surface with his waver, and he desperately shoved it down again.

"Trust me," she urged.

Stars above, he wanted to, but it felt terrifying to surrender to her, not knowing what plan there was, if any, whilst that denizen roiled under his skin.

"I trust you," he said, and held out the dagger.

VENYA PUSHED CLOSE TO HIM, grasping the hilt with him, her hand over his. Her heart thundered so loudly it was all she could hear over the roar of magic, that orb inexorably closing in around them.

This would need to be precise. All of it. It all hung upon the blade of a knife.

She saw the tension in every strained muscle of his body, his shaking shoulders, the set of his clenched jaw. He was in pain, battling the demon inside him. They had but moments before he would be overwhelmed once more and lost forever.

"Now! Do it now and get us out of here!" she cried, and pressed a punishing kiss against his lips, even as she tugged *hard* on that weave of light magic, collapsing it inwards.

Kass's hand moved, dragging hers with it. He turned the shadow blade upon himself, stabbing upwards from his abdomen into his chest. She felt his cry shudder through their joined lips as the blade bit deep. His fangs grazed her lip, drawing blood. The iron tang tasted of the promise of life and the threat of death.

Kass crushed her close with an arm around her, trapping that dagger between them, and wrenched them away into smoke and wind.

CHAPTER FIFTY-THREE

Kass felt the tear in his soul. The demon was fused so deeply with him, rooted so deeply in the very depths of his being, it felt as though he tried to sever a mountain from the bowels of rock. That blade of shadow did not cut his mortal flesh, and yet the pain of it stole his breath away. All that anchored him were his lips upon hers. The taste of blood in his mouth.

This blade pinned a part of him there and he balanced upon the precipice between life and death. To cut too far this way or that meant death. The life and warmth of her fixed in his earthly arms gave him the courage he needed to shove the blade all the deeper and sever to the very core of what bound him and the demon Ozul together.

Kass wrenched the blade down in a savage cut. He was not sure if he screamed, or the demon, or both of them. He gathered what little remained of his strength, and pulled himself and Venya away, feeling viciously, victoriously hollow as the power of that golden orb snapped closed behind them.

MERE FEET THEY TRAVELLED, catapulted out of the stone circle onto the banked snow outside. Venya landed atop Kass and rolled off. She groaned at the impact, for it jolted her already battered body, but forced herself to her feet. Kass lay immobile in the snow, his mouth open, eyes closed.

"Kass!" she screamed, but he did not respond. At his side, his hand uncurled loosely, the handle of the dagger in the snow beside him, its blade spent.

From within the circle, an unearthly shriek emanated, one that jarred her bones and made her teeth ache. She wheeled around. That orb had shrunk so far now that she could only just see the dark shape trapped inside the web, railing against the power that bound it. The demon. Free. Given corporeal form, but not for long.

Venya dropped to her hands and knees and crawled to the stone sentinel where her pack still lay abandoned. She opened it and reached inside, scrabbling until her hands bumped the chain. She wrenched it out.

The wind whipped her breath away—an unnatural wind, born of a maelstrom of dark and light magic fusing and tearing, dangerously volatile.

Smaller the orb shrank, encasing the writhing darkness. Spokes shot out, dark spears lancing into the night, trying to escape. And each time, the web of golden light pulled them back in. With every second that passed, the screams of the denizen trapped inside grew, as it could no longer avoid the painful burn of that light against its darkness.

Venya crawled on her hands and knees, bracing against the growing inferno of magic. It jolted her bones, sending a fizzle across her skin that felt akin to being stung and burned and drenched in ice water all at once, so powerful was the battling magic there. She found one end of the chain, her hands slipping and fumbling, so cold and tired were they, and wound her fingers around it.

This was it.

She flicked the chain towards the writhing orb, now just the size of her head, and let go. Attracted to the orb's magic, that chain wrapped around and shrank with it, the two ends of the chain fusing.

That shriek from within faded, and the storm with it, until only silent carnage remained, with Venya in the eye of the storm that had finally ceased raging.

Resting in the snow, as big as Kass's clenched fist, was that golden orb, its surface solid, bound by a shimmering chain no wider than her finger. No trace of the darkness could she see or feel inside it, the demon inside utterly contained. She trembled and fell to her hands and knees in a moment of relief, as the stars fell overhead.

Kass.

She turned. He had not moved.

A bolt of fear shot through her. She pushed to her feet and sprinted to him, slipping on the mud—the melted snow, churned up by the energy of the magic.

"Kass!" She sank to her knees beside him, lifting his head onto her thighs. She hovered a hand before his lips. Breath fluttered out, weak but warm. A pulse thumped in his neck, steady and reassuring.

Alive. He was alive.

They both were.

As she sent the last trickle of her magic into him, she sensed no darkness. Only Kassimir.

She bent over him with relief, just as his cracked voice uttered her name.

"Venya…"

She had never been so glad to hear it from his lips.

It was *over*.

They were both alive.

The demon was gone.

And they had survived Starfall.

CHAPTER FIFTY-FOUR

"Ah." Kassimir winced as Venya dabbed at the cut on his forehead. He did not remember how it had come to pass.

"It's clean," she murmured. With a tingle of gentle magic, she ran a thumb across his brow, healing it. "There you are."

"Thank you." He captured her hand in his and pressed it to his cheek, inhaling the scent of her, appreciating that they were both alive. And she was there with him.

He had healed her first, using the strength of the wellspring, and then taking from it again to spirit them back to the safety of his castle. Sitting on his drawing room floor before the fire, the larder downstairs raided for food, for they were both starving, she had insisted on repaying the favour once they had devoured every morsel.

Kass was tired to his bones and yet the lightest he had felt in centuries. That black stain weighing down his heart, dragging him into the abyss, was simply… gone. He felt weightless without it. Kass pulled her close, resting their foreheads together, and in silence they huddled on the rug, letting the warmth of the roaring blaze beside them soak into the depths of his finally whole and unsullied heart.

Let this peace never end.

HER STOMACH FLIPPED at their proximity, his hand still pressing hers against his cheek, his coarse beard tickling her palm, his scent of leather and musk, amber and sweat wrapping around her. Venya could feel the absence of the demon stripped from him, the lightness in him was so visceral. They had not bound it in a grimoire as they had planned, but perhaps the alternative was better. A grimoire was altogether too independent and wily.

Captured in the orb of light and bound by her magical chain, Kass's first stop was to place the apple-sized glowing construct into a chest sealed with the most powerful of magic. One that he had promised to bury in a place so impenetrable the demon would never escape to endanger the world of Altarea again. For now, he had settled for a warded vault below the castle.

Starfall continued outside, pinpricks of light shooting across the sky visible through the tall windows. They had not come to marry after all on that night under the terms of their initial arrangement. But neither had they perished. The odds had seemed so impossible and yet, they had survived.

Every part of Venya ached with tiredness, her mind dull and slow. She was in no rush to move. She could have happily slept on the rug at that point—but there were pressing questions to answer. She pulled away from Kass, tipping her head to one side to regard him.

"What now?" Hurt threatened to spill into her chest and carve through the settling euphoria and relief.

"We sleep," he said hoarsely, "and I will not be parted from your side."

Her stomach swooped at those words—and the promise in his loaded gaze. She wished for both.

"I must return to Pelenor," she said, dropping her gaze. That hurt threatened to breach inside her, torn by the impossible decision she now had to make.

"Immediately?"

Venya swallowed. *Yes.* "I must go to my mother. It has been too long."

"I understand. You need to see she is well with your own eyes."

Venya nodded, her throat too clogged to speak.

"Forever?"

She could not answer.

"Do you want to leave?"

Venya shook her head and covered her face with her hands, for that was the truth of it. Despite everything that had passed... she wanted selfishly to remain in this haven with him.

Kass prised her hands away from her face, dropping a kiss into each palm. "Then don't." His voice filled with a pleading note.

She whispered, "I have to." *Why does this feel like tearing myself in two?*

"You do not have to do anything you do not wish to, Venya. You know that is true. You have spent your life in service of others—no more. Serve yourself. Surely, you cannot consider anything but your oaths and burdens fulfilled."

"They would miss me far too much, and my job—"

"They would make do without you. If you make your choices from guilt, fear, or obligation to others, you will live only a life of regret. Believe me. I know that. You deserve happiness on your own terms." He squeezed her hands.

She swallowed.

"Venya… we have achieved the impossible this night. By rights, we both ought to be dead. You saved me from a fate worse than death—one I have been trying to escape for centuries—and in mere weeks, you achieved the impossible. Whatever this is between us, it is powerful enough to defy fate. If you want this, me, choose it. *Choose us.*"

"And turn my back on all I know?" Hot tears pricked at her eyes. She wanted this for herself, but… *do I want it more than I need to serve others? Do I deserve it?*

"If you want to. You can build a new life for yourself—here, with me. What would make you happy?"

You. This. She groaned.

"I can see it inside you, what you want—and you fear it, don't you?"

Her eyes slipped shut, but she could not avoid the truth of his words. *He understands me better than I understand myself.*

"Yes."

"Take what you want. I will not force you, but I will state my position. Your choice remains your own. I have never felt like this before. I want *you. Here.* By my side. I offer everything I am, everything I have to you, now and forever.

"Go home if you need to—I should like to come with you, if you do, for I mean it when I say I do not wish to part from you—but return when you are done. Become the lady of my lands. Together, think what we could do. You could be mistress of your—our—private grimoire collection. I know your lands forbid their making, but I see the curiosity within you at my magic."

Her eyes opened at the smile that broke through the fervour in his voice.

"I know you know it to be true. They can be created and used for harm, like constructs, but they can also be created and used for good. Would that not be incredible? To have the freedom to pursue such magics—together?"

Become the lady of his lands? Pursue such magic together? "What are you asking me?"

That smile turned serious. "Venya, you are free to come and go as you please, but I ask you to return to me. To call this your home. I ask you… to marry me. For real."

Her lips parted and her breathing hitched. *What…?* How much had changed since the last time he had uttered those words. Then, she had wanted nothing more than to flee such a choice. Now she wanted to run towards it. *When did that change?* She had not quite realised the cumulative weight of all those small moments between them.

"There is no rush whatsoever. We can have as long an engagement as you please. I shall ask your father's permission—whatever you require of me—as long as I am yours and you are mine, because I never wish to be parted from you. I owe you my life and my freedom, and I desire nothing more than to worship you every day for the rest of our long lives. Everything I am is yours, Venya."

Her chest soared with the elation that ran through it, a heady feeling that threatened to carry her away. Would the Athenaeum continue without her? *Yes, certainly.* She was one librarian amongst many. Would her mother, her parents, be fine without her? *Yes, certainly.* With her mother's health returned, they would have no need of her.

What do I want? A new adventure. One that she chose for herself, following the truth in her heart, unfettered by guilt or obligation, burden or duty. Something fluttered in her chest, a caged bird longing to be free.

What do I choose? Myself. Him. Us. This.

"Yes," she breathed.

Yes, to a new adventure she had never expected—as Venya de Rochefort, consort of Kassimir the Dark.

THE END

EXPLORE VENYA'S WORLD

Read the completed Darkness of the Living Forest trilogy for more from Venya's world.

Access extra content from *Married By Starfall* (character art, maps, extra scenes and more!) and sign up to Megs Reader club for all the latest news at www.megcowley.com.

AUTHOR'S NOTE

Dear readers,

Hello and welcome back to readers old and new! Thank you so much for reading *Married By Starfall*. If you're a long-time reader, I hope you enjoyed another expansion of the story that began so long ago with dear Harper and dark Dimitrius in the *Chronicles of Pelenor*, continued with your favourite elven thief Aedon in the reader-demanded series *Tales of Tir-na-Alathea* which first featured Harper and Dimitri's daughter Venya…and all the way to here. *Married By Starfall*.

I was not finished telling Venya's story, and now I can rest easier. She featured in a much smaller part than I intended in *Tales of Tir-na-Alathea*, and I always felt her business unfinished! So, I am very glad that I got to return to walk in her shoes, feel her heart, and write her story, touching in with her years later in her journey through life, when she was quite ready for a change (even if she didn't know she needed it!).

This is the first true romance I have written. After finishing drafting the last of the *Tales of Tir-na-Alathea* story,

I was utterly spent and genuinely terrified of never being able to write another word again. In stepped Venya. Shy, calm, patient, hopeful Venya. She took my hand and showed me those grimoires she so loved. A tower room with a rib-vaulted ceiling from which sprawled a new little nook of the fantasy world I have lovingly built for fifteen years already. And the face of a dark fae sorcerer who lived in snowy mountains under a star-filled sky

Kassimir was born—hair in a knot, wounded heart, and all. And suddenly I had the spark of this story and I had to tell it. It consumed me. It took a year to coax some life back into the flame of my creative well, but this story turned that ember into a blaze of phoenix-like incandescence that wrote itself in mere weeks. This story brought back my love of writing romantasy and I am so thankful for that.

I dearly hope you enjoyed it and that you love Venya and Kass too. I hope you were satisfied by every part of this story —for that's my dearest wish as a storyteller, to make you feel wonderful things.

If you're not quite ready to leave them just yet, please do visit my website www.megcowley.com. Every book/series I write is accompanied by extra content for you to access there from maps to character art to bonus scenes. For *Married By Starfall*, there's all of the above, including a steamy version of chapter 37 for those of you who like more heat, and an extra happily-ever-after epilogue showing a little of what came after "the end" for Kass and Venya. I hope you'll enjoy them and they'll be the cherry on top of the cake.

You can also sign up to my newsletter there to receive exclusive behind the scenes news and all the latest updates, or follow me on social media.

If you're new to my work and want more, I have several completed series that I think you'll like—particularly the

Chronicles of Pelenor, a gripping epic romantasy quartet telling the tale of Venya's parents Harper and Dimitri and their troubled road to love in the midst of world-ending evil, and also the *Tales of Tir-na-Alathea*, a darkly delicious romantasy trilogy that picks up some years later and introduces Venya for the first time amidst the cast of characters in her first years as a librarian training at the Athenaeum of Pelenor.

Happy reading!

Warmest wishes,
Meg
August 2022

ACKNOWLEDGMENTS

Thank you so much to everyone involved in the production of this book—and everyone who reads it!

I'm sincerely grateful to my fellow authors Angela J. Ford, Jenny Hickman, Sarah K.L. Wilson, Tessonja Odette, Barbara Kloss, and Brianne Wik for making this such a joy-filled creative endeavour. This project made me fall back in love with writing fantasy and romance all over again.

Thank you to my dear friend Clare Sager. Your faith and enthusiasm helped me find the courage to write this story from my heart.

Thank you to my editor Hanna for helping polish this manuscript to a sparkle worthy of reading, and for my incredible assistant Hannah for her tireless work to bring this all together into a spectacular immersive experience on and offline.

Thank you very much also to my readers who volunteered names for the demon in this story. To Georgiana who chose the eventual final name "Ozul", congratulations and thank you! And, honourable mentions to one of my longest-serving and dear readers Mandie and my friend Sarah for suggesting names that were very close runners up!

And, thank you to all of my readers. I appreciate your grace, patience, support, and love, as you waited for me to write something new.

ABOUT THE AUTHOR

Meg is a *USA Today* bestselling fantasy author from England, where she lives with her husband, young son, and two mischievous cats.

Meg writes sweeping romantic fantasies filled with betrayal, intrigue, high stakes, and guaranteed HEAs. She adores writing dark brooding book boyfriends, feisty heroines, and found families, She has several completed romantasy series all set in the same world. Her favourite trope to write is enemies-to-lovers.

Meg's favourite past times are reading and hiking. She can usually be found curled up with a cup of tea and a riveting fantasy romance book, or out walking the wild, windswept moors of Yorkshire dreaming up her next story.

Visit www.megcowley.com to find out more, discover Meg's books, find exclusive reader bonus content, and join her reader's club newsletter.

www.ingramcontent.com/pod-product-compliance
Lightning Source LLC
Chambersburg PA
CBHW070548310726

48982CB00011B/1505/J